Lady Alexandra's Hunt

A Regency Romance

Sydney Salier

This is a work of fiction. The characters, locations, and events portrayed in this book are fictitious or are used fictitiously. Any similarity to real persons, living or dead is purely coincidental and not intended by the author.

ISBN: 9798464829237

To Michael

As always, thanks for the inspiration

CONTENTS

1 Homecoming ... 1
2 Memories ... 8
3 Arrivals ... 16
4 Settling in ... 24
5 Letters ... 32
6 New friends ... 39
7 London Seasons 1803 ... 46
8 Return to the country ... 55
9 London Seasons 1804 ... 63
10 Worthington Ball ... 72
11 Meetings ... 80
12 Friends old & new ... 88
13 Discoveries ... 96
14 Showdown ... 103
15 Recovery ... 110
16 House-party ... 117
17 Conversations ... 125
18 Confrontation ... 132
19 Courtship? ... 139
20 Winter of discontent ... 148
21 Reciprocity ... 155
22 Advice ... 162
23 Acceptance ... 169
24 Conclusion ... 177
Books by Sydney Salier ... 182

1 *Homecoming*

1801

The Hunts were a peculiar family. As far back as anyone could trace, each generation had ever only one son. Some generations had one or more daughters, but in each generation, there had only been a single son to carry on the family name. The daughters generally married into prominent families and in their turn produced several children of both sexes.

Everything went well until the current generation, where there were two children. Sixteen-year-old Lady Alexandra Hunt and her younger sister Daphne, who was fourteen. There was no brother to carry on the family name.

There would never be a brother since both their parents had been killed in an accident the year before.

Her uncle, the Earl of Marven, as the husband of her father's only sister, had been their guardian. Now he too was gone. He had been much older than his wife, but had appeared in good health, until the previous evening, when he had collapsed and died. The doctor said he had had a problem with his heart.

~~H~~

The following morning Lady Beatrice, the Countess of Marven, sought out her niece, 'we need to speak.'

When they were both comfortably settled in her private sitting room, Lady Beatrice asked, 'How much do you know about the politics of your current situation?'

'Do you mean the fact that Cousin Frederick has inherited the title of the Earl of Marven since you do not have any children?'

'That is part of it. The part that concerns me the least. My main concern is how it pertains to you. I am afraid that if we stay here when Frederick takes possession of the estate, he will try to force you into a marriage with him. I suspect he would not take no for an answer since by marrying you, he thinks he would get two earldoms instead of one.'

'Do you truly think he would be so unscrupulous?' Alexandra was sceptical. She remembered meeting her cousin once, about five years earlier. He had seemed haughty and dismissive of the young girl she was at the time. But most adults she knew had no interest in children.

'From what I know, the assets he is inheriting will barely cover his debts. He is five and thirty years of age, and he is still unmarried since no sensible father will allow his daughters anywhere near him. He is also a known gambler and a rake.'

Lady Beatrice sighed. 'I feel sorry for the tenants and the servants here. They will not have an easy life with him in charge. Unfortunately, the law is on his side. As the nearest male relation to my husband, he inherits the title and the entailed estate.'

'But surely, not everything is entailed,' protested Lady Alexandra. 'I cannot believe that Uncle would not minimise the damage Cousin Frederick could do.'

'You are correct. Everything that is not entailed will come to me. That is why my own position does not give me any concern.' Lady Beatrice smiled fondly at her niece.

'But now we come to the crux of the matter. Do you know the conditions of your father's title and will?'

'I know that grandfather was worried over the fact that there has ever only been one son in each generation in the family. Father told me that grandfather petitioned to have the patent modified, to allow a daughter to inherit if there is no male candidate from the immediate family. Marrying into the family does not qualify a man. I know that when I reach my majority, I will inherit the title, which I can then pass on to my oldest son, if I have one. Otherwise, it will pass on to my oldest daughter. And if I have no children, the title can go to Daphne or her children, preferably male, or female if she too has no sons.'

'You will not inherit the title on your majority.' When Alexandra looked startled, Lady Beatrice explained, 'it is already yours. We have simply kept that quiet to protect you. As it stands, you already are Lady Alexandra Hunt, the Countess of Herne.'

'Oh... dear. I had not expected this. I thought I had a few more years to learn what I need to know.' Now Alexandra looked truly concerned.

'Rest easy, my dear. Although the title is yours already, the patent stipulates that until the holder of the title is eighteen, he or she will require a guardian, or regent, if you prefer that term. We planned to tell you about this next year, to allow you to get used to the idea that on your eighteenth birthday you will be in charge. This will include guardianship of your sister. Although if you are wise, you will keep quiet about it and let people assume that you will be under guardianship at least until your twenty-first birthday.'

Lady Beatrice smiled encouragingly. 'Gregory was well qualified to look after your interests as far as your estate was concerned. But with his death, I am left to be your guardian and I think it best if we work together because I am not the manager that my husband was. But between what your father and my husband taught you, what I know and with the help of your steward, I am certain we can manage.'

Alexandra thought about her aunt's revelation for a few moments. 'Thank you, Aunt. I agree that would be best. Since I have no brother, father *had* started to teach me about estate management. But there is much I do not yet know.'

She sighed before suggesting, 'But could we relocate to Herne Hyde? I think it would be good for me to go home. There you can teach me to be a proper Mistress, or is that Master, of Herne Hyde.'

'That is the spirit,' smiled Lady Beatrice. 'I already gave orders to start packing. I would like you to leave as early as possible, tomorrow by preference. I want you out of reach when Frederick finds out about Gregory's death and shows up for the funeral and the reading of the will.'

'You are that concerned about him?'

'I married the only decent man in the whole Marven family,' declared Lady Beatrice. 'I do not trust any of the others. And since you are just barely old enough to get married without too many raised eyebrows, you are in danger while you stay here.'

Lady Beatrice smiled and patted Alexandra's hand. 'You can leave tomorrow with my companion, Mrs Hodges. I will follow immediately after the reading of the will. In the meantime, do not be surprised if several carts and carriages with my belongings arrive at Herne Hyde.'

At last, her well known impish smile made a reappearance. 'You will also inherit several pretty maids. I am confident that with both of us in residence in your home, the extra hands will be welcome.'

'I believe our housekeeper, Mrs Martin will find positions for them,' Alexandra agreed, also smiling conspiratorially. Then another thought occurred to her. 'What about Daphne? She is supposed to return from her visit with the Cartwrights in a fortnight.'

'I think it best if I make a detour on my way to Herne Hyde, to collect your sister.' Lady Beatrice suggested and Alexandra concurred.

'There is one more thing you need to know. If anything should happen to me, I have nominated the Earl of Matlock to be your guardian. He is an honourable man and will keep you safe.'

'Are you truly this much concerned about Cousin Frederick?' Alexandra was now truly shocked.

'Not at all,' her aunt reassured her. 'But accidents can happen on the road, and I wanted you to know who to turn to, if anything should happen. There is nothing more sinister than ordinary concern for my favourite nieces.'

Alexandra huffed, 'Daphne and I are your only nieces. But I thank you for your concern and foresight. Although, if I am to leave on the morrow, I should see to my packing.'

'Do not worry if you forget anything. I will be very thorough in checking that nothing is left behind,' assured Lady Beatrice.

~~H~~

The following morning, just after dawn, Lady Beatrice farewelled her niece. 'Safe travels and I will see you in a week or two,' she said while hugging the girl.

'I am certain Mrs Hodges will take good care of me, as will all those footmen you insist on sending.' Alexandra looked ruefully at the number of servants who were to accompany her.

'You are precious to me. Take care.' With a final pat on the hand, Lady Beatrice urged her niece to enter the carriage where Mrs Hodges and Sally, Alexandra's maid, were already waiting.

Sally helped her mistress to arrange a travel rug over her lap. While the temperatures during the day were mild, this early in the morning there was already a nip in the air, a harbinger of the autumn which had just started.

As soon as the ladies had settled, the coach started moving.

Lady Alexandra turned to Mrs Hodges. 'I am sorry we had to drag you out of bed at such an early hour,' she said to the lady, who she knew was not at her best in the morning. 'I will not be offended if you wish to sleep since I brought a book to keep me company.'

Mrs Hodges, a comfortable looking lady of middle years, smiled gratefully. 'That is very considerate of you, My Lady. It was rather late when I was able to seek my bed last night.'

'Think nothing of it. It will be two very long days on the road before we reach Herne Hyde. I am certain we will all sleep as much as we can, to speed the journey. You too, Sally,' she advised her maid.

'Thank you, My Lady. But I am wide awake at the moment. I will just get on with my knitting if you do not mind.' Sally was a young woman in her early twenties, a petite blonde with a bubbly personality and a love for fashion. Her needlework was exquisite, and she was grateful that she was allowed to subtly embellish her own dresses when she was not busy with Lady Alexandra's.

The embroidery she added to her mistress's gowns was bolder but elegant, which suited the young lady's moderately tall and slim build.

Lady Alexandra had been a pretty girl and over the past year had just started to grow into her beauty. Her features had begun to lose their childish softness to become quite pert. Combined with her auburn hair and hazel eyes she would attract considerable attention when she came out into society.

'Suit yourself,' she told her maid with a smile. She then pulled out her book and began to read.

~~H~~

It was a gruelling journey. Even though the roads were dry, and they could make good speed, the almost constant bouncing of the carriage, which even the best springs could not prevent, was wearying for the occupants.

They only made brief stops to change horses, which everyone used to stretch their legs and take care of their other needs.

They assuaged their hunger from a generous basket of food they had brought along. At noon they stopped just long enough for the ladies to have a cup of hot tea before setting off again.

They eventually stopped for the night just before full dark.

The head coachman, Samuels, informed Lady Alexandra, 'we made excellent time today. God willing, we should be at Herne Hyde in time for tea tomorrow.'

'I hope they will not be surprised by my return,' mused Alexandra.

'Lady Beatrice sent a message yesterday to inform your staff of your return. And I have been instructed to send an express in the morning to confirm our expected time of arrival. Knowing Mrs Martin, she will have a good dinner ready for you,' he smiled at his young Mistress.

~~H~~

Samuels was correct on both counts. They arrived at Herne Hyde in time for a sumptuous tea and Mrs Martin informed them that dinner could be served at the usual time.

After briefly refreshing herself and enjoying some tea and the cakes Mrs Martin had arranged for, Lady Alexandra headed upstairs to go to her room for a much-needed bath and a rest before dinner.

She was intercepted by Mrs Martin before she could enter her accustomed room. 'My Lady, I have taken the liberty to have your new rooms freshened up. I hope you will like them,' she said as she guided Alexandra to another door down the hall.

When Mrs Martin opened the door, Lady Alexandra was stunned, 'that is the Master's suite,' she gasped.

'It is your suite, as is proper, since you are Master of the estate,' explained the housekeeper.

Alexandra swallowed hard as she tentatively stepped into the room. She was reluctant to occupy her father's rooms, fearing too many memories. She was surprised by what she found. 'You have completely redecorated the room. It looks wonderful,' she smiled at Mrs Martin.

'I am very happy that you like it, My Lady. I based this on your previous choices, although just a little more grown-up. If there is anything you would like to change, just let me know.' Mrs Martin was pleased that her surprise had worked so well. She smiled as she curtsied and then left the young lady to explore her new domain.

Alexandra had entered into the Master's sitting room. A door to the right led to a study, where a desk stood in front of one of the large windows with a view of the approach to the house.

On the other side of the sitting room was the bedroom which had windows facing both east and south. This in turn led into her dressing room and then to a room her father had experimented with.

A bathing room. It contained a copper in one corner, which not only heated the room but also the water for the bath. The servants were very much in favour of the arrangement since they did not have to carry cans of hot water from the kitchen, up the stairs, to fill the bathtub. The tub was even connected to a pipe which allowed the water to drain out.

Beyond that room, was a small room which had previously been used by her father's valet and now housed Lady Alexandra's maid, Sally.

Sally was currently in the dressing room unpacking the trunks. She beamed at Lady Alexandra, 'these are grand rooms. And you are going to love the bathtub. It has a wonderful view of the garden.'

Alexandra laughed, 'in that case I had better make use of that view.'

~~H~~

2 *Memories*

That evening, after Alexandra changed into a nightgown and robe, she curled up on the window-seat of her study.

She let her eyes wander around the room, which now looked so different from the room she remembered. While she was grateful to Mrs Martin for making the changes, to allow her to claim the space which had been her father's domain, as her own, a part of her missed how it had once been.

Or to be more honest, she missed her father. Alexandra had had a good relationship with her mother, but as the heir, she had spent more time in her father's company, than her mother's, or even her sister's.

Most of her earliest memories were of her father in this room, when he had patiently answered all her childish questions.

~~H~~

Another snippet of memory intruded.

Her father riding to inspect the estate, with Alexandra perched in front of him on his favourite gelding. But despite the fact that the feeling of her father's arms about her made her feel secure and comfortable, Alexandra had objected to being nothing but a passenger. She pleaded to have her own horse.

Soon afterwards, the Earl presented her with a pony, and taught her to ride. She smiled at the memory of how proud she had felt to be independent.

From then on, whenever there was no urgent need for speed, Alexandra had accompanied her father on his activities.

~~H~~

Over the years, the pony had been replaced by progressively larger and more spirited horses, until her father presented her with her own stallion, whom she named Pegasus, for her thirteenth birthday.

It had been a timely present, as only a few days later, on their return home from inspecting the furthest field from the house, a fierce storm had blown up unexpectedly. Only the speed of their mounts had allowed father and daughter to outrace the worst of the tempest.

They had dashed into the stable yard, still at a full gallop and only barely managed to slow, to enter the stables, where they had sheltered until the worst of the storm had subsided.

Alexandra remembered the camaraderie she felt, while she and the Earl sat on haybales, trying to calm their horses, and listening to the wind howling outside, making conversation impossible to hear. Yet his arm across her shoulders and the comforting squeeze of his hand, conveyed more than mere words could.

~~H~~

Since Alexandra had shown an interest in the estate from an early age, the Earl encouraged her curiosity. It was not until she was twelve years of age, that she discovered the reason for his attitude.

Lady Herne revealed that the birth of Alexandra's sister had been exceedingly difficult for her, and, as a consequence, she would be unable to have any more children.

That day Alexandra learnt that she was her father's heir.

Concerned that he might be disappointed at not having a son, she asked her father that question.

'I do not regret it in the slightest. In you I have found the best of both. You have the aptitude to make an excellent Master of Herne, but you are also a charming young woman. How could I repine to have such an heir?' The smile he gave her had nothing of regret, only pleasure and pride.

Alexandra had rushed into her father's arms and given him a fierce hug. 'Thank you, father. I promise I will do my best to always make you proud.'

~~H~~

From then on, the Earl had included Alexandra in all his business dealings with his steward, the tenants, and his man of business. Even on the occasion when he had negotiated to purchase another estate, situated only eight miles from Herne Hyde, which was for sale because the heir had squandered his livelihood in the gaming hells of London.

The young man had blustered at the inclusion of Alexandra in the negotiation, until the Earl cut him off. 'Lady Alex is my heir. It is only right for her to learn how society functions. If you do not wish to sell your estate to me because of that, you only need to say so.'

Since the man had been desperate for the funds, he grudgingly agreed. A deal was struck, and the Earl added another estate to his holdings.

Once the transfer was complete, the Earl had taken Alexandra to the estate, and provided her another shock. 'I wish you to look over the estate and tell me what should be done with it. If you can make it profitable, I will sign it over to you.'

'You mean that you want me in charge of the restoration?'

Her father had given her a challenging grin. 'If you do not feel that you are up to it…'

'No, Father. I will make this the best estate you have ever seen,' Alexandra enthused.

Mr Uphill, the steward, who had struggled to maintain the estate despite the constant drain on funds, was rather dubious when the Earl told him that Lady Alex, then only thirteen, was to be in charge. In the end he claimed, 'I suppose the Lady cannot be any worse than my previous Master.'

The steward accompanied father and daughter on a tour of inspection and pointed out the most urgent repairs. He was amazed when Alexandra enquired, 'is there any reason, other than lack of funds, why you have not drained those bottom fields?'

'Lack of funds is the only reason, My Lady.'

'Then why did you not mention that drainage is a problem?'

'Because Mr McGill always said it was not worth the expense to drain those fields. He would not be able to recoup the investment.'

'Probably not in one year, but I would expect in the second year the drains would pay for themselves.'

Once she had established what she wanted to do, the Earl advanced Alexandra the funds she needed for repairs, as well as installing the drainage in the low-lying fields. For several months, Alexandra, accompanied by two large footmen, made almost daily trips to the estate which she renamed from Darrowdale to Dianadale.

Within the first year, Alexandra was able to repay her father half the advance, and keep enough funds back, for other improvements to the estate.

Two months before the accident, which claimed the lives of her parents, Alexandra repaid the last of the advance, and the Earl transferred the estate into Alexandra's name.

It was the proudest day in both their lives.

~~H~~

Outside it started to rain. The noise of the raindrops hitting the windowpane roused Alexandra from her reverie.

She realised that she had become chilled, sitting next to the window. Giving the room a final look, she made her way to bed. The warm brick towards the foot of the bed, made her grateful for her thoughtful staff.

~~H~~

The following day, after a good night's sleep, Alexandra sent for the steward immediately after breakfast. She met with him in the study on the ground floor.

'Mr Brown, it is good to see you again. How is that new system of crop rotation working out?' Alexandra was eager to hear if the ideas she had discussed with her father just before his accident were successful in implementation.

'My Lady, it is good to have you home, although I was extremely sorry to hear about the death of your uncle. He was a good man.' He hesitated for a moment. 'Unfortunately, he was quite conservative. He did not permit us to fully implement the new system, although I was able to try it out on the home farm.'

He now sported a big smile, 'we had a twenty percent increase in yield.'

'I would say that proves our theory. You may go ahead and use that on the whole estate.' Alexandra was ecstatic.

Mr Brown was a little more hesitant. 'Will there be any opposition to this plan?'

'I hardly think so, Mr Brown. My aunt is my new guardian. While she is an excellent choice as the guardian of a young lady, she is no farmer. She believes in letting experts get on with their expertise. Now tell me everything that has been happening in my absence.'

For the rest of that day and several days following her arrival, Lady Alexandra was either closeted with her steward or riding the estate, to see at first-hand what her steward had reported. She also visited each of the tenants, who were happy to see the young Lady back in residence.

During those days she also made time to visit Dianadale. While she had corresponded with the steward, he was pleased to see her and show off all the improvements he had been able to accomplish in the last year. Alexandra congratulated him on his achievement. The crusty man waved off her compliments, while complaining about the dust that made his eyes water.

~~H~~

Eventually she felt she was up to date with estate matters and at last took time to spend an afternoon in the parlour, to have tea with Mrs Hodges.

That lady was in an ill humour. 'Lady Alexandra, I know it is not my place to tell you what to do, but I would suggest you take up your duties as Mistress of the estate, rather than to go gallivanting about. I have tried to fill in for your neglect, by discussing menus with Mrs Martin and ensuring that the house is properly run.'

'There was no need for you to do that. Mrs Martin knows I will eat whatever she has the cook prepare and she has run the house quite successfully for nearly twenty years. If she needs any direction, Mrs Martin will ask me.' Alexandra was nonchalant.

Mrs Hodges huffed, 'do you not know anything about being Mistress of an estate?'

'Obviously not as much as you would like me to, Mrs Hodges. But I was not raised to be the Mistress of the estate.'

'How can any lady of quality not learn the duties of a Mistress?' Mrs Hodges asked in high dudgeon.

'Because I was raised to be the Master of Herne Hyde.' Lady Alexandra was getting rather irate at being taken to task for doing her duty.

Mrs Hodges was nonplussed. 'Oh... I forgot. It just seems so unnatural. Young ladies are supposed to concern themselves with feminine accomplishments, not running all over an estate.'

'For your information, I was not running all over the estate, as you put it. I was not even gallivanting about. I was busy visiting the tenants, which is the duty of both the Master and the Mistress of the estate. My tenants get the benefit of both in one visit.' Lady Alexandra calmed down and tried to placate the lady. 'Cheer up, I am here now and ready to speak to Mrs Martin.'

Just then, Mrs Martin entered the room with a tea tray for three people.

'Mrs Martin, I see that you have time to join us for tea.' Alexandra smiled at the newcomer. 'This is a much more civilised way to catch up on what is happening.'

Mrs Martin set the tea service and the plates with cakes on the table and said with a smile, 'I am gratified that you are following your mother's example and display the same condescension which she did.'

Lady Alexandra happily accepted the thanks and the compliment from the housekeeper. 'It always was a pleasure to take tea with you and mother,' she replied. She did not add that in her opinion Mrs Martin, despite being a housekeeper, had exquisite grace and manners, and would have been a credit to any drawing room of the *ton*.

Alexandra poured tea for each of her companions while suppressing any sign of the glee she felt at the reaction of Mrs Hodges.

To Mrs Hodges' surprise, Lady Alexandra fixed her cup exactly as she liked it and according to the smile on Mrs Martin's face, her cup was perfect too.

'My apologies, Lady Alexandra. Maybe I was a bit too hasty in my opinion earlier.'

'That is quite all right, Mrs Hodges. You do not know me as well as Mrs Martin.' Alexandra smiled, then she turned to the other lady.

'I wanted to thank you for rearranging the study. It made working in it much easier, without being constantly reminded of my father.'

'You are welcome, My Lady. I am happy that you approve of the changes I made.'

'Do you have to be so formal, Mrs Martin. What happened to Miss Alex?'

'Miss Alex grew up and has become Master of the estate. It would not be proper for me to use your childhood name.' Mrs Martin smiled to ensure that Lady Alexandra understood her change in address was out of respect.

'Very well, I shall accept that in public. But when in private would you be prepared to compromise and call me Lady Alex?' Alex smiled winsomely.

Mrs Martin could not refuse the request and agreed, 'mind you, only in private.'

'Very well, I shall now be all grown up and ask, have the new maids arrived?'

'An hour ago, nine maids from the Marven estate arrived, together with quite a lot of luggage. I have taken the liberty to have everything that was marked as Lady Beatrice's personal effects, put into the Mistress' suite...'

'Good. I was going to ask you to do just that. Are there any of my things as well?' asked Alexandra, because she had realised, she had forgotten some books.

'There were two trunks for you. One contained items which had obviously just been laundered, the other was marked as personal, to be opened only by you. That one I had put into your study.'

'I will look into it presently.'

'I am grateful that Lady Beatrice warned me of the influx in staff. It saves me from having to hire anyone to take care of the extra work now that you will all be living here. The lady also sent a letter detailing the capabilities of each, based on her housekeeper's evaluation.' She handed the missive to Alexandra with a smile.

'It appears we have gained some very highly qualified staff. Will that cause any problems since, I presume, they will not be able to have the same kind of positions here for the moment,' Lady Alex mused.

'Jenny, the head parlourmaid was quite emphatic. They are happy to do any kind of work, as long as they know they will be safe from being importuned by a libidinous master,' explained Mrs Martin with a grin. 'Her words, not mine,'

Alexandra chuckled, while Mrs Hodges blushed and tittered.

'It seems that is settled satisfactorily. Now we just have to await the arrival of my aunt.'

They discussed ideas that Mrs Martin put forward to improve the house, most of which Alexandra was happy to approve.

Afterwards Alexandra repaired to her study to examine the contents of the second trunk, which contained not only her missing books but also the ledgers her uncle had maintained for her estate. As she expected, they had been meticulously kept and justified every single expense.

~~H~~

3 Arrivals

Two days later an express arrived, announcing the arrival of Lady Beatrice the following day.

The lady and her maid arrived in the late afternoon in high spirits. Their coach was followed by several hired carriages.

Alexandra had stepped outside to greet her aunt and was surprised to see the convoy, which continued on, to the side of the house.

'Welcome, Aunt. It appears you have brought us some guests,' she greeted the lady. 'But where is Daphne?'

'It seems the poor child became distracted while she was reading in the garden and was caught in a shower. Currently she is abed with a nasty head cold. While it is not too serious, Mrs Cartwright thought it safer if your sister stayed in bed for a few days. They will deliver her to us next week.'

She gestured towards the convoy. 'As for the rest, I hope you do not mind putting them up for a few days. I could not leave them to Frederick's not so tender mercies,' explained Lady Beatrice with a smile. 'I will tell you the full story as soon as I have refreshed myself.'

Lady Beatrice was as good as her word. In short order she had washed off the dust of the road, changed into a clean dress and come to the sitting-room. On the way she had collected Mrs Hodges, Mrs Martin and Mr Martin, the butler.

'I think I will tell you the whole story from the beginning, based on the reports I had from various people,' said Lady Beatrice to her niece, when she had settled with a cup of tea to quench her thirst.

'The day after my husband's death, our solicitor, Mr Thompson came to see me. He had instructions from Gregory to oversee the removal of my inheritance from the estate, to ensure that I received everything my husband had wanted me to have. He was accompanied by our

Magistrate, Mr Carsons, who offered to witness and notarise that I only removed my personal possessions and the items on the list. He also brought the list of bequests.

By the time you left, the packing of my property was well in hand, and the bequests had been bestowed or sent to the recipients. I sent everything, other than some clothing, two days after you left. The maids whom I sent to you were the hardest working staff I have ever encountered since they knew that they would travel with my goods.' Lady Beatrice grinned at the memory.

'As it turned out, we could have taken more time, as Frederick only deigned to grace us with his presence a full week after your departure.'

~~H~~

Frederick strode into the house. 'I wish to view my cousin's remains,' he demanded without greeting or courtesy.

Lady Beatrice, who had just stepped into the foyer, followed by Mr Carsons, the local magistrate, replied, 'My husband Gregory, the Earl of Marven was buried two days ago.'

'How dare you did not wait for my arrival,' blustered Frederick.

'The weather was too warm to wait on your convenience. Since you could not be bothered to show respect to my husband by attending promptly, I saw no reason to delay his funeral.'

'I was busy attending to affairs,' Frederick exclaimed in a haughty tone.

I bet you were, thought Lady Beatrice, but aloud she said, 'since you are here now, we can get on with the reading of the will.'

'Send the solicitor to me after breakfast. I wish to rest and refresh myself before attending to business.' Frederick turned to the butler, 'you may escort me to the Master's suite.'

'Certainly, Sir. This way if you please.' The butler bowed politely and indicated the way.

When Frederick entered the Master's suite he was affronted because it had been stripped of all personal items of the late Earl.

'What is this? This looks like a monk's cell, not the suite of an Earl. What happened to all the decoration?' Frederick fumed.

'His Lordship left instructions for his suite to be cleared so that his successor could decorate it to his own taste,' the butler explained.

Frederick looked around in disgust but decided to live with it until he could imbue the rooms with the grandeur he deserved.

'Very well, you may leave. But have a bath prepared and send me a bath attendant.'

The butler bowed himself out of the room with a politely murmured 'certainly, Sir.'

When the bath had been prepared and his valet had helped him undress, Frederick received yet another unpleasant surprise.

'What are you doing here?' he asked the big, burly man in his forties. 'And where is my bath attendant?'

'I am Brian, your bath attendant,' replied the man politely, without the slightest indication that he thought the situation amusing.

'I expected a female bath attendant,' growled Frederick.

'I am sorry, Sir, but she only attends the Countess,' replied Brian.

'I do not care, send her to me,' came the shouted demand.

'Sir, you should be aware that that particular woman is my mother.'

Frederick looked horrified. 'Why would I want to bed a crone?'

'Why indeed?'

'You insolent cur, you are fired without a reference!' Frederick shouted and lashed out at the man with his fist.

The man swayed slightly, and the fist missed its mark. 'Thank you, Sir,' was the unruffled reply as the man quickly left the room.

Frederick picked up a pitcher of cold water and threw it at the man's retreating back. It hit the door just as it closed.

~~H~~

The next day, Frederick had a leisurely breakfast at what he considered a civilised hour. By the time he finished, it was noon and he had kept Mr Thompson and his two clerks, who were on hand to ensure the reading of the will would go smoothly, cooling their heels for three hours.

Although Mr Thompson and Mr Carson, the magistrate, had been visiting with Lady Beatrice for the whole morning.

When Frederick decided he was ready, he was directed to the library, where everyone was waiting for him.

When he walked into the room, Lady Beatrice greeted him with a sarcastic, 'so good of you to join us.' She then introduced the solicitor, the magistrate, and Mr Thompson's assistants, before saying, 'now let us get down to business.'

Frederick protested, 'Cousin Beatrice, it was good of you to entertain these gentlemen, but you may now leave. We have business to discuss.'

Mr Thompson protested, 'the late Earl of Marven specifically instructed that the Countess of Marven should be present at the reading of the will.'

'She does not have the mind to understand business,' complained Frederick.

'If the Countess should have an issue in comprehension, which I doubt, I will offer an explanation,' said Mr Thompson.

'Very well, she can stay,' Frederick *graciously* conceded.

When Mr Thompson read out the conditions of the will, Frederick became incensed. He had assumed that everything in the manor was part of the entail and when he found out that the particular artworks he had been planning to sell, were not to be his, he tried to bully Lady Beatrice into leaving them behind.

He became furious when she handed him the notarised list of items she had removed.

'How do I know that you did not take things which are not yours to take?' Frederick growled.

Mr Carson spoke up, 'As the magistrate, I was asked to be an independent witness. I checked off every item on the list. The Countess meticulously only took items to which she is entitled. Everything else is here. To suggest anything else is to impugn her honour. Also known as defamation, which is punishable by law. Even peers are not exempt.'

Frederick grudgingly accepted the injunction but could not resist to have a petty revenge. 'Cousin Beatrice, since you have removed your possessions already, you can now remove yourself from Marven Manor as well.'

Then he seemed to have an afterthought, 'but before you go, send your nieces to me. They have been most remiss not to have presented themselves to me already. It is time they met their new guardian.'

'What gives you the idea that you could be the guardian of Lady Alexandra and Lady Daphne?' asked Mr Carson.

'As head of the family, I am the only one qualified for that office,' replied Frederick pompously. 'And if one of them pleases me, I shall make her my bride.'

'Apart from the fact that since both Ladies are too young to be out in society, your demand for a bride is obscene, you, My Lord, are not the head of the Hunt family. You are the head of the Marven family. Therefore, you are not qualified to be their guardian,' huffed Mr Thompson. 'The late Earl appointed a new guardian and several alternatives, if the first choice becomes unavailable. You are not on that list.'

'There was no mention of the guardianship in the will,' protested Frederick, ignoring the slur about his wish for a young bride.

'The guardianship was not related to the estate and was dealt with in a separate document,' explained Mr Thompson without betraying the satisfaction he felt in thwarting the new Earl.

'I wish to see that document,' demanded Marven.

'I am sorry, My Lord. But you have no right to demand access to the personal documents of another family completely unconnected to you,' Mr Carson pointed out.

'Apart from that, you are too late. the Ladies have left the estate,' Lady Beatrice said as she quit the room.

~~H~~

Alexandra laughed, 'oh dear, what condescension. Make me his bride, indeed. But I should be safe. I have no intention of pleasing him.' Then she bristled. 'But the idea that he would consider my little sister, who is only fourteen years of age…' She shook herself in disgust.

'The only pleasing things about you that he cares about are your looks, wealth and title,' cautioned Lady Beatrice. 'He does not care about your character or personality. And even your looks are secondary to your wealth.'

'I stand corrected,' conceded Lady Alexandra. 'But the story thus far does not explain that convoy of carriages.'

'I was coming to that. Since Frederick effectively threw me out of the house with nothing but the clothes I was standing up in, Mr Carsons kindly offered to put me up for the night. He thought it was too late in the day to start a journey.

What Frederick was not aware of, since he slept so late, was that the rest of my things were already packed and loaded, and my maid Dorothy was awaiting me in the carriage.

The other thing he missed was that Brian had come to me, asking for a reference from me since Frederick had fired him without one. While I spoke to Brian, he mentioned that due to the treatment he had received, it had caused great concern amongst all the staff. Apparently, they did not feel safe working for their new employer, who was prepared to use his fists simply because his desires could not be satisfied. I offered references to anyone who wanted to leave.'

Lady Beatrice smirked. 'That may have been a mistake. I spent the morning approving references for staff who have family in the area and therefore, somewhere to go. Mr Thompson's clerks were very helpful, not just in preparing the references for me to sign, but also calculating and documenting the severance pay for everyone. Luckily, the household funds on hand were sufficient, although barely, to pay out everyone who wanted to leave.

The ones without families pooled their resources to hire any conveyance they could get hold of.

I am told Frederick overindulged again that night and did not notice the exodus which occurred at dawn the next day. To the best of my knowledge, he still has a valet. Even the carriage he arrived in had been hired since he expected to use the Marven carriage, which is much better than the one he used to own.'

'Good grief. Are you telling us that the new Earl has that big manor house and not even a cook?' exclaimed Mrs Martin.

'Terrible, is it not?'

~~H~~

The following week, late one afternoon, saw the arrival of the final member of the small family. Lady Daphne Hunt was being returned to her sister by Mrs Cartwright.

As soon as the carriage stopped, without waiting for a footman to place the steps, Daphne jumped out and rushed to her sister to engulf her in an enthusiastic hug. 'You cannot imagine how much I missed you, Alex.'

'Can I not? You forget that I too was without my favourite sister.'

'I am your only sister,' huffed Daphne.

'Therefore, it follows that you are my favourite,' Alexandra completed their private joke.

'I am glad to see you back at Herne Hyde,' declared Mrs Cartwright, who had exited the coach much more decorously. 'Although I am saddened by the passing of the Earl of Marven. He was an excellent man.'

Mrs Cartwright was a distant cousin of the Hunt family, and her daughter Amelia had gone to school with Daphne, where they had become close friends. The school had been necessary for Daphne since neither of her parents could satisfy her hunger for knowledge.

After their parent's passing, Alexandra had been busy learning all that she could from her uncle, to prepare her for her role as Master of the estate, thus Daphne had been glad of the support from Amelia and her family. And though she refused to admit it, Daphne had found the Earl to be rather irritating.

Yes, the Earl had been a true gentleman and respectful towards his wife, yet being rather traditional, he could not comprehend that his young niece was more intelligent than most, if not all, of the men he knew. The Earl had struggled to accept that Alexandra was the heir to the Earldom, but since she had the courtesy not to rub his nose in her more masculine accomplishments, the Earl had come to a grudging respect for the young woman and fulfilled his duty by teaching her.

But Daphne was altogether different. She had a brilliant mind, but the arrogance and impatience of youth, untempered by social skills. Daphne had no problems pointing out in minute detail any misconceptions he might voice. The Earl in return had tried to force her into what he perceived to be the proper female role. To keep the peace, Daphne had spent much of the last year at school or visiting with the Cartwrights, whose daughter Amelia was similarly gifted, although not as abrasive.

Now that the Earl was gone, Daphne was glad to be reunited with her sister.

'Mrs Cartwright, I cannot thank you enough for the care and support you have shown to my sister. Perhaps, if it is agreeable to you, Amelia could spend some time with us at Herne Hyde.'

Mrs Cartwright laughed. 'My dear Lady Alex, I would be delighted to have Amelia come and stay with you. I should probably not say so, but it would be exceedingly pleasant for my family not having to try to keep up with Amelia for a time.'

'Surely, Amelia and I are not that bad,' pouted Daphne.

'No, child. But whilst you are both wonderful girls, it is exceedingly tiring for us lesser mortals to comprehend how your minds work.'

Lady Beatrice, who had joined them, suggested pointedly, that they would all be more comfortable inside the house.

~~H~~

4 *Settling in*

1801

After quickly cleaning up from the journey, the ladies all met in the small family parlour. Lady Beatrice engaged Mrs Cartwright in conversation, allowing the sisters to have a quiet word.

'Are you happy to be home, Daphne?' Alex asked in concern. 'Will you not miss your friend?'

Daphne took her sister's hand and squeezed it. 'Alex, I enjoy Amelia's company, since she is the only person with whom I can talk without fretting if she will understand what I am saying. But she is not you. You are the only close family I have left. While I cannot discuss science with you, you are the only one who understands me. About how I feel. Amelia still has both her parents; she does not know how bereft one can feel when that support has been removed.'

She shook her head with a small grimace. 'Mother, Father and you could never quite understand my interest and passion for science, but you always accepted and supported me. With you I am come home.'

Alexandra squeezed her sister's hand in return. 'I too am glad to have you back, and for exactly the same reasons. Other than the part about science, of course.'

'Of course, and although I cannot understand your passion for estate management and business, I too accept that about you.'

'But speaking of science, if you wish to remain at home, rather than going back to that school, we can hire tutors for you.'

Before Daphne could respond, dinner was announced.

'I will come and speak to you later,' Alexandra promised, before leading the party to the dining room.

~~H~~

As promised, when Daphne was getting ready for bed, Alexandra joined her in her room.

Alexandra was a little uncomfortable when she explained in a rush. 'Mrs Martin changed father's suite to make it suitable for myself, and since Aunt Beatrice is acting as the Mistress of the estate, I had her installed in mother's suite. I do not want you to feel as if I deliberately excluded you, or that you are not important, or that...'

'Alex, stop. I like my rooms, and I have no wish to move. I understand that as the new Countess, you need to occupy the Master's suite. But since nothing has changed for me, I can stay in the rooms in which I am comfortable.'

'You do not mind?'

'Of course not. As long as you do not deny me access to the library, I shall be perfectly content in my old rooms.' She looked around her domain. 'Although... I think it is about time that I had a more grown-up look.'

'Whatever you want changed, it is yours,' Alexandra promised, relieved that Daphne was so very sensible.

'I would like a bathing room like father had installed...' Daphne looked hopefully at her sister.

'You shall have it, and since such things interest you, you shall manage the installation.' Alex grinned as her sister threw her arms around her neck.

'You are the very best of sisters. I cannot wait to have a thoroughly hot bath... in a warm room, no less.'

Alexandra returned the hug with equal fervour.

After enjoying the closeness for a while, she pulled back a little and asked, 'did you think about whether you want to go back to school or have private tutors?'

'I think private tutors would be best. Teachers in school always react badly when I point out their errors during class.' Daphne sighed. 'It is most frustrating to discover how little teachers actually know.'

'Perhaps when you become proficient in a subject, you should write the textbooks from which they could teach,' Alexandra joked.

Daphne beamed. 'That is a most excellent idea, Alex. I always knew that you were brighter than you looked.'

Alexandra rolled her eyes. 'I thank you for the compliment. I think.'

Once the major questions were dealt with, the sisters exchanged the news which had not made it into their letters, until Daphne was ready to go to sleep. At which point, Alexandra retired to her own room and started to make plans for their future. She did not get very far since sleep overtook her too.

~~H~~

Mrs Cartwright returned to her family after spending the night at Herne Hyde. She did promise that Amelia would be allowed to visit during school holidays. Alexandra suspected that although Mrs Cartwright loved her daughter, she too found it difficult at times to deal with an exceptional young woman.

At Alexandra's request, Lady Beatrice, who had acquaintances in many areas, wrote letters requesting recommendations for suitable tutors for Daphne.

'You do know that many men will have an issue with teaching a young woman,' Lady Beatrice commented to the sisters.

'I know, but I think it will be easier to find a man who is liberal minded enough to teach Daphne, than find a bluestocking who is educated enough to perform that office.'

In the end, the ladies decided not to limit their search by the sex of the tutor.

Over the next few weeks, they received the names of half a dozen potential candidates.

To save time, Lady Beatrice invited them all to Herne Hyde for a visit.

~~H~~

Five men and one woman arrived at Herne Hyde within a few hours of each other and were greeted by Lady Beatrice.

After the last arrival had refreshed himself, the party assembled in the drawing room, where Lady Beatrice introduced them to her ward, whose sex she had conveniently forgotten to mention in her letters, since Daphne had insisted that she would be able to convince her potential tutors of her abilities, if given a chance to speak to them.

The reaction of three of the men was as expected. 'You want me to teach a young woman? Are you bereft of your senses? Women are mentally incapable of grasping the concepts of science. I have better things to do than waste my time on a female,' spluttered Mr Freeman, the oldest of the objectors, sentiments which were echoed by Mr Morgan and Mr Regan.

'Gentlemen, I have an interest in science. If you feel incapable of imparting knowledge of the physical world to a student, perhaps you should consider a different career,' Daphne challenged them.

'Miss Donaldson, gentlemen, my niece's abilities are not in question here. You have been invited to be examined, to discover whether you are capable of expanding my niece's knowledge,' Lady Beatrice intervened to cut short the brewing argument.

'Who is to be our examiner?' asked Miss Donaldson, trying to suppress a smirk. She found it amusing to watch the men being put in their place.

'Lady Daphne will conduct the examination. After all, she is the most qualified to judge your competence.'

Alexandra, who was sitting quietly in the background, observed the candidates with interest as Daphne started to question them.

Soon there was a heated discussion between all of them. Interestingly, Daphne seemed to spend much of her time observing the others, only occasionally interjecting her own comments. But it soon became clear that her sister could hold her own in the arguments.

Alexandra noted that after the initial excitement, which Daphne had displayed, she became increasingly irritated and dejected.

Mr Freeman stormed out of the room in a huff, when Daphne proved that his knowledge was incorrect because it was out of date. The male students he had taught over the last two decades, had accepted his teaching without ever once challenging him. To think that a mere slip of a girl had bested him in a scientific debate was unbearable to his self-esteem.

The others concluded that Lady Daphne, merely from reading every book or paper on science which she could get hold of, was almost as knowledgeable as they were, and there was little that they could contribute to the furtherance of her education.

~~H~~

'That was a complete waste of time,' sighed Lady Beatrice, after the last of the visitors left. 'To think that these people are the ones to teach the next generation, fills me with despair.'

'Apart from Mr Freeman, at least they were willing to further their own education. They were not content to rest of their laurels, and spout nonsense which was already disproved twenty years ago.

Daphne suddenly grinned. 'I think that if you can find a natural philosopher, who wishes to engage in research, but does not have the funds to do so, he might be willing to allow me to participate in his work.'

'But he would not be teaching you.'

'It seems that I have already learnt much that is known at present, the only way to learn more is to discover something new. I would learn from observation and discussion of his work.'

Lady Beatrice looked dubious, but conceded, 'I suppose that we could try this approach.'

The following month, Mr Harrison, a young scholar who had just finished his degree at Oxford, was installed at Herne Hyde to conduct his research into heat and electricity. Having three older sisters, he was prepared to accept a female research assistant.

Within weeks, Alexandra rarely saw her sister, since she was too busy with her studies, and having a wonderful time. Daphne's happiness was complete, when Amelia Cartwright joined her at Herne Hyde, and soon became an integral part of the research. After a few more weeks, there was no question of Amelia returning to her family, other than for occasional holidays.

There was only one fly in the ointment. Many of the experiments involved chemical reactions, some of which created smells none at Herne Hyde were prepared to tolerate. The research had to be put on hold, until a laboratory could be constructed far enough from the house, so as to not inconvenience the residents.

~~H~~

The months flew past while Lady Alexandra learnt to become Master of the estate and deal with all associated business.

While Lady Alex, as she liked to be called, was not of age, technically her guardian, with advice from the steward, was in charge of the estate.

In reality, Lady Alex was the undisputed Master. Her father, the Earl, had laid the groundwork by discussing business and his plans for the estate with his daughter. Now Mr Brown was advising the young lady, but she was the one making the decisions. Mr Brown was happy to have such an apt student.

When he commented on the fact, Alexandra admitted to having gained experience at Dianadale.

It was a relief to Alex that her aunt had taken on the duties of the Mistress of the estate, as far as the running of the house was concerned, especially since Daphne had no interest in either role.

Now that a Mistress was in charge of the house, Mrs Hodges had quite happily settled back into a supportive role, being helpful rather than officious. Alexandra was grateful for the change.

The tenants on the other hand, were quite happy that Lady Alex combined both roles in one visit. The men spoke to her about issues with the fields or livestock, while the women kept her abreast of any problems with the homes.

Mr Brown was amused that everyone had started to call her Lady Alex. The shortened version of her name gave it a slightly masculine flavour, which was more appropriate for the Master of the estate, while the honorific of Lady ensured that her sex was never in doubt.

~~H~~

One afternoon, when Lady Alex was coming back from riding out to visit a tenant, she encountered Tim Smith, one of the under-gardeners, accosting Jenny, one of their new maids.

Lady Alex had noticed Tim before because he was an exceptionally handsome young man. Whenever she had encountered him, he had been properly deferential to her. Now, with no sign of deference, he appeared to be pressing Jenny for favours which she was unwilling to provide.

'No, Tim. I have no interest to be the latest victim to your desires,' Jenny protested.

'You had better give me what I want, or I will ruin you. I have Mrs Martin eating out of my hand,' he sneered.

'Mrs Martin might believe you, but I do not,' said Lady Alex while she stepped into view, just as Jenny kicked Tim in the ankle and tore herself away from him.

The maid rushed to Lady Alex's side while Tim whirled to face his Mistress. 'My Lady, this is not what it seems. This little tart has been leading me on ever since she arrived here. I was just trying to get her to show her true character.' He smiled in his most winsome fashion which had always worked on people, particularly women.

Lady Alex looked first at him, then at the maid who looked both disgusted and apprehensive while shaking her head. 'You have indeed succeeded in forcing Jenny to show her true character,' replied Lady Alex with a disgusted smile. 'You have also succeeded in displaying your own. You are fired. I will not have any man importuning my female staff.'

She noticed Mr Brown coming around the corner of the house. 'Mr Brown, I have just fired Tim Smith for trying to force himself on Miss Jenny. Would you please ensure he has left the estate before nightfall.'

Her steward looked initially startled, but this turned into a satisfied smile when he agreed to do his Lady's bidding. He had had his suspicions about Smith, but never had any proof of wrongdoing.

~~H~~

Alexandra went to have tea with her aunt and asked Jenny to send Mrs Martin to join them to discuss the issue, after assuring herself that the maid had taken no harm from the episode.

When all the ladies had their cups of tea, Lady Alex asked her housekeeper, 'Mrs Martin, what do you know about Tim Smith?'

'Tim Smith? He seems like a nice industrious young man. Because of his looks he is rather too popular amongst the female staff. They appear to throw themselves at him. The poor thing seems constantly beset by amorous maids.'

'I encountered him earlier in company with Jenny,' Alexandra said, curious what her housekeeper's reaction would be.

'Do you mean to tell me that even Jenny cannot resist a pretty face? I had thought better of her,' exclaimed Mrs Martin.

'Your faith in Jenny is justified. When I encountered them, she was fighting off Tim Smith.'

'*She* was fighting *him* off?' Mrs Martin was shocked. 'I thought that the girls were always throwing themselves at him because he is exceedingly good looking. Although I was not comfortable with the fact that he did not try very hard to resist them.'

'Nevertheless, when I saw him, he was threatening Jenny with ruin, if she did not grant him her favours.' Alexandra paused, observing Mrs Martins shocked expression. 'He said he had you eating out of his hand.'

'I admit to a certain soft spot for him. He always seemed to be put upon because of his looks. You know, he always had that lost little boy look...' Mrs Martin sighed, 'although I sometimes did wonder whether he was using his looks for his advantage. I would have believed Jenny, if she had come to me with her side of the story.'

'Either way. It is not an issue for us anymore. I have fired him,' Alexandra explained. 'But I was very impressed with Jenny. The way she handled him. She was very competent at protecting herself.'

Mrs Martin smiled at that comment. 'You have my husband to thank for that. He used to be a sergeant in the army before he entered service. When those maids from the Marven estate arrived, he took it upon himself to teach them how to foil unwanted advances.'

Lady Alex appeared thoughtful for a moment. She looked questioningly at her aunt who had stayed quiet during the exchange. At an encouraging nod from Lady Beatrice, Lady Alex asked, 'I wonder if he could teach me...'

~~H~~

5 *Letters*

While Lady Beatrice was in mourning for her husband, it allowed her and her nieces to avoid overly curious neighbours.

This gave Lady Alexandra time to grow into her role as Countess of Herne, Master and Mistress of Herne Hyde.

Contact to the outside world was mostly limited to correspondence from family and friends. In the case of Alexandra, more of the former, while her aunt received more of the latter.

One of the letters Alexandra received was from her great-aunt Felicity, who had been the younger sister of her grandfather. The previous Earls of Herne had avoided her company as much as possible. Based on the correspondence Alexandra was reading, she could understand the reason.

Dearest niece

I hope this letter finds you in good health.

It has come to my attention that your aunt Beatrice has taken over guardianship of yourself and that you have gone to live at Herne Hyde. Far be it from me to question the decisions of both your father and the Earl of Marven, but your great uncle, Viscount Durham, feels it would be more suitable for you to move into our home until your marriage, an event I feel certain you will not delay, since the line of Herne must be preserved.

To that end I have several suggestions of suitable young men for you to consider. Foremost among them is my husband's dear nephew Randolph, who is the second son of the Earl of Braxton. He is eminently suitable to take over the reins of managing the estate, allowing you to take your rightful place as the Mistress of Herne Hyde and mother of the future generation of the earldom.

I agree with my husband that you should marry as soon as possible, to prevent Herne Hyde from deteriorating, for lack of a master to firmly hold the reins. You will require a new Earl to bring the estate back to its former glory. The Viscount has already spoken to his nephew, who has declared himself willing to take on the responsibility of the Earldom.

Living with us until your seventeenth birthday, will give you the opportunity to get to know your future husband with the utmost propriety. Then you can be presented as the wife of the Earl of Herne, and nobody will question your title as his Countess.

Since your father always claimed you were a sensible girl, I am certain you will see the advantage of this arrangement. Therefore, please confirm your date of arrival as soon as possible, so that I can have your room ready for your occupation.

Your great-aunt

Lady Felicity Stone, the Viscountess of Durham

Alexandra was torn between amusement and fury when she read this epistle over breakfast that morning. The nerve of that woman, whom her father and grandfather had detested as the most stupid and grasping woman in all of England, to think that she could order her great-niece's life to her own advantage.

Alexandra was aware from her father's complaints that the Viscount of Durham was a poor manager of his estate and always in debt. She therefore suspected that Lady Felicity would expect her nephew to recompense her for the introduction and sponsorship of the match.

Then the humour of the situation won out. Dear Aunt Felicity thought she could be pressured into marrying in just six weeks. It was preposterous.

Lady Beatrice, who shared the meal with her niece, noticed Alexandra's distraction and enquired to the cause.

'It seems Cousin Frederick is not the only one interested in making a match with myself,' replied Alexandra, looking at her aunt with wry amusement. She passed the letter to her aunt. 'I wonder how many others will have similar ideas.'

Lady Beatrice quickly scanned the letter and smirked. 'They expect you to be an ordinary girl of sixteen. In other words, they think you have been trained to think only of feminine accomplishments, fashion, and how to catch a husband as quickly as possible. They also think you to be easily led – preferably to the altar by the man of their choice.'

After a moment's thought Lady Beatrice said to her niece, 'this comes at an opportune time. I have been meaning to speak to you about your potential marriage and your coming out in society next year.'

'Aunt, please do not push me to get married just yet. I am still learning to run the estate properly. I do not have time to waste on a husband,' protested Alexandra.

'Quite the contrary, my dear,' laughed her aunt. 'I wanted to warn you to be careful and not to rush into anything.'

Alexandra was stunned. 'Everyone from grandmother down, has been telling me that I must get married as soon as possible and produce an heir for Herne.'

'I am fully aware of that. But I believe they do not consider the situation properly. You are in an almost unique position. I know of only one other woman, Henrietta Godolphin, the second Duchess of Marlborough, who was a peeress in her own right, just as you are a Countess in your own right. That brings with it a great deal of responsibility, the least of which is to produce an heir.'

Lady Beatrice smiled at the mixture of disbelief and relief on her niece's countenance.

'All those clucking hens seem to forget that you are responsible for hundreds, if not thousands, of people. They see a pretty young girl and think of their own youth and expectations. Marry and have children.'

Lady Beatrice chuckled when she remembered all those missives which she had received from various family members, imploring her to encourage Alexandra to enter society immediately and to marry at the earliest opportunity.

'I sincerely hope that you will marry and have children – eventually. But you must find a husband who is content to have a minor role in the business of the Earldom. Even when you marry, the title is yours. Your husband will not share in it. Considering the law of the land, which effectively makes slaves of women...'

'I know things are bad for women, but we are not slaves,' Alexandra interrupted.

'When they marry, women become the property of their husbands. If a person is property, that, by definition, makes them slaves. Even her property becomes his. As long as a man does not kill his wife outright, at least not in an obvious manner, he has the right, by law, to do whatsoever he wishes – force himself on her and turn her into a broodmare, even lock her up and beat her.'

When Alexandra looked like she wanted to protest again, Lady Beatrice sighed and said, 'let me finish. I was trying to make a point about the law and your unusual position.' She patted her niece's hand.

'Generally, after marriage, a woman and her property become her husband's property. This will not apply to you. You will need to find a man, who can accept that you must be at least his equal. Your property will remain yours, to pass onto your heir, as will be the responsibility to look after it. I hope you can find someone who can support you.

Many men will flock to you because they will assume that they will gain control of your wealth. They must be made aware that the patent specifies that the heir, who is you, will remain in control until the title and the estate are passed onto the next heir, at the death of the incumbent. The heir must be your child, it cannot be your husband.

You now have several options.

If you are exceedingly lucky, you will find a man whom you can love and respect, and who loves and respects you in return. A man, who will be content to be your consort and assist you in your role as Countess.

If you are not so lucky, and I must warn you that it is unlikely you will find such a man, look for a man with whom you at least share a mutual respect. A man who can give you the heir you need... after the wedding, of course.

If all else fails, you might wish to consider allocating an amount as a dowry, which you can hand over to your husband at your wedding. In return he provides you with an heir, and then minds his own business.' Lady Beatrice grinned, 'it is not called the marriage mart for nothing, you know.'

'Now you wish *me* to become a slave owner... by buying a husband,' giggled Alexandra.

'Not at all, you impertinent little rapscallion. I wish for you to be one of the lucky few and achieve the first option - a long and happy marriage with a loving husband and several children. I merely mentioned it as a last resort.'

'Very well, Aunt, I will be careful and not rush into anything. I will not let a pair of fine eyes and a handsome figure tempt me into an ill-advised marriage.'

'You have my full confidence to choose wisely.' Lady Beatrice smiled at Alexandra.

She then gave a mirthless chuckle. 'What do you plan to do about this invitation?'

Alexandra thought for a minute before making a decision. 'I think it only polite to respond to the letter and make it quite clear that according to the law, my future husband will not be the Earl. That should slow down the potential suitors who are primarily after my title.'

After breakfast, Alexandra penned her reply.

Dear Great-Aunt Felicity

I thank you for your kind letter and I hope my response finds you in the best of health.

I am afraid that I must decline your generous offer.

I could never ask your nephew to demean himself, if we were to be married, to be introduced as 'The Honourable Mister Stone' while I am being introduced as 'The Countess of Herne'. This is due to a change to the patent, at the request of your brother about five and thirty years ago, of which you seem to be unaware. Since then, the title is entailed to heirs of the body, rather than heirs male, and therefore, the heir always holds the title, not the husband, if the heir is female.

Because of that change, my husband will never be the Earl of Herne. Since English law stipulates that a woman is granted the courtesy title of the husband, but a husband is not granted the courtesy title of the wife, if she has the higher rank, your nephew would always be known as 'The Honourable Mister Stone'.

I am convinced that you will understand that I could not possibly ask this of your nephew, who, I am sure, has too much pride to tolerate being subordinate to his wife.

I must also decline your kind invitation to visit, since I am currently engaged in learning how to manage my holdings. As I am certain your husband can testify, there is much to be learnt about the effective running of an estate. Because I must honour my father's wishes and apply myself to my education to the best of my ability, I cannot spare the time for other distractions.

Your great-niece

Lady Alexandra Hunt, the Countess of Herne

Her aunt chuckled in amusement when she was offered to peruse the letter. 'That should keep some of the hounds at bay. I wonder if she knew about the title and hoped that you did not. And I must congratulate you on your choice of words regarding the Viscount's knowledge of running an estate.'

~~H~~

Lady Beatrice's correspondence was more congenial, even though her first letter was from her solicitor.

Dear Countess Marven

I hope this correspondence finds you in good health.

I have no wish to trouble you, but I must advise you that the new Earl of Marven is trying to contest the will of your late husband.

The new Earl tried to retain my services, but I had to decline because it would constitute a conflict of interest.

You may find it of interest that, since the Earl was unable to find any staff to work at the Marven estate, he has relocated to his townhouse in London. He may find another solicitor there, but you can rest assured that your husband made certain that his will is unbreakable.

Your faithful servant

Peter Thompson. Esq

A few days later, Lady Beatrice received a letter from a friend in London, which, amongst other gossip, included some amusing information.

I have some delicious news to relate to you concerning the new Earl of Marven.

Apparently, he arrived in town last week, only to find that all the staff at the townhouse had resigned from service before his arrival. The only one left in the house was the old butler who welcomed the Earl in the foyer, handed him a set of keys, bowed, and walked out the front door.

He, the butler, lives now in pleasant retirement with his oldest daughter, who married a rather wealthy tradesman.

In case you are concerned, all the former staff have found new positions in good households. I should know.

I understand that in the meantime, the Earl was able to hire some inferior help. I believe he frequently eats at his club.

Lady Beatrice chided herself for being unchristian when she could not resist a chuckle.

~~H~~

Miss Amelia Cartwright sent a letter to her mother.

Dear Mother

I am having the most marvellous time with Daphne and Mr Harrison.

Would you believe that Alexandra had a laboratory built for our use? That is in addition to a standing order she placed with Hatchard's, to send us the latest books on science. She has even arranged for us to visit Camborne in Cornwall later this year, so that we can see Mr Richard Trevithick's steam-powered locomotive. I believe that Lady Beatrice has an interest in mining. It is amazing whom the lady knows. As you keep telling me that you have no head for science, I shall not bore you with details of our work, other than to say it is most exciting.

I am grateful that you and father consented for me to come and live at Herne Hyde. I love you even more for your understanding.

Your loving daughter, Amelia

~~H~~

6 *New friends*

1802

Lady Beatrice had accepted an invitation by Lady Markham to come for a visit to Cambridge. The two ladies had met at school and had become firm friends. Their friendship had survived nearly three decades.

'I am exceedingly pleased that you were able to accept my invitation. I am also delighted that you brought your niece.'

'I thought it would be a good opportunity for Alexandra to dip her toe in the water, so to speak. She will have her presentation in a few months, followed by her first London Season. Here she will have the chance to attend a few small functions, before the madhouse that is society in London.'

'Sound reasoning. Although the assembly at the University next week will not be exactly small, considering the number of students attending. But it will be much more informal than London. Although I would suggest a certain amount of caution. Some of the students tend to be rather wild. They think because of their heritage they are entitled to whatever they want.'

'I will be careful, Lady Markham, and only dance with gentlemen whom you have introduced. I presume you know which of the gentlemen will behave with decorum,' offered Alexandra.

'That is a wise decision, my dear, and yes, I know whom to trust.'

~~H~~

'Ah. Here is one of the Denton doubles,' said Lady Markham to her companions. They had arrived at the ball the university was hosting only a few minutes earlier. 'I am convinced you will enjoy his company. They have lovely manners.' The lady attracted the attention of a handsome young man, who approached and smiled at Lady Markham.

'Robert Flinter at your service, Lady Markham.'

'Thank you, Lord Robert, for identifying yourself. I would like to introduce to you two dear friends of mine. Lady Beatrice, the Countess of Marven and her niece Lady Alexandra Hunt, the daughter of the Earl of Herne. Ladies this is Lord Robert Flinter, second son of the Duke of Denton.'

'I am enchanted to make the acquaintance of such charming friends of Lady Markham,' said Lord Robert with an elaborate bow.

'I too am pleased to meet you, Lord Robert,' Lady Beatrice responded with a smile at his extravagant address.

'It is a pleasure to make your acquaintance,' Lady Alexandra said while she curtsied. She tilted her head to query, 'although I am puzzled why you needed to identify yourself to Lady Markham, if you are acquainted with our friend?'

'To my great misfortune, I am often confused with my twin brother Alistair, the Marquess of Denmere,' explained Lord Robert. He placed a hand dramatically over his heart. 'Although I cannot for the life of me understand how that can be, since I am the much more handsome of the two of us,' he added with twinkling eyes.

'I suppose that explains the soubriquet Denton doubles,' Alexandra laughed, amused at the antics of the young man.

'Now that my identity has been established, may I be so bold as to enquire if you have any dances available?' he asked of Alexandra.

'We are just arrived and since you are the first gentleman Lady Markham deigned to introduce, all my dances are available.'

'How fortunate for me. In that case, may I have the honour of the next set, Lady Alexandra?'

'You may indeed, Lord Robert.'

~~H~~

Lady Alexandra enjoyed the company of Lord Robert. His mannerisms, while extravagant, were obviously meant to be seen for what they were, simply some light-hearted flirtation.

His conversation was quite delightfully lacking any mention of the weather. When she made an off-hand comment about preferring the company of people with sense rather than position, her dance partner exclaimed, 'Lady Alexandra, pray tell how you come to the exceptional attitude of not caring for rank?'

'My father taught me to be more interested in a person's character than their station. I find that to be excellent advice. It should help me to avoid fortune hunters when I officially come out in the next London season,' Alexandra explained.

'Your father must be an exceptional man. I admit, I quite agree with you. According to my brother, fortune hunters of either sex are the bane of our existence.' Lord Robert sighed theatrically. 'I would much rather be a poor but happy second son, than a miserable heir trapped into a marriage I did not choose.'

Instead of pointing out that her father was deceased and she herself held the title in her own right, Alexandra replied sympathetically, 'It must be very difficult for your brother then.'

'Indeed, it is. It is difficult enough for myself since some people mistake me for my brother. Whenever they do, I am subjected to the same fawning that he has to endure.

'You poor man,' laughed Alexandra, 'to have to endure the attentions of many beautiful and accomplished young ladies.'

'Please do not laugh, My Lady. You just wait until *you* have to endure descriptions of the weather for six hours straight,' protested the gentleman.

'Touché,' acknowledged Lady Alexandra, wondering how she would stay awake in London society.

~~H~~

Lady Markham, aware of Lady Alexandra's inexperience with society, had made a point of only introducing her to young men whom she knew would be pleasant company and respectful to the young woman.

Because the assembly was being hosted by the university, there were more gentlemen than ladies present. Therefore, Lady Alexandra kept busy, dancing every dance.

She was having a wonderful time dancing but realised that Lord Robert had been correct in the level of conversation she could expect. Eventually she needed a break from discussions of the weather and sought the ladies retiring room to refresh herself as well as rest her feet and mind for a few minutes.

When she returned to the ballroom, she was intercepted by two young men before she could return to her aunt's side.

The more handsome of the two men bowed and said, 'My Lady, my friend and I have been admiring you all evening. We are both hoping we are not too late to secure dances with you.'

Alexandra was surprised that the men would approach her directly, rather than ask to be introduced by Lady Markham. She looked at the speaker and his friend and found that the second appeared like he had had too many visits to the punchbowl.

The first man, while apparently handsome and charming, had an air about him that was oddly familiar even though she had never met him before, and it set her teeth on edge. She suddenly realised he reminded her of the undergardener, whom she had fired for importuning one of the maids.

'I am sorry, sir, I cannot dance with you since we have not been formally introduced,' Alexandra said as she tried to sidestep the men.

The man blocked her and in his most ingratiating manner said, 'My Lady, one does not need a formal introduction in a ballroom simply to dance. Please do me the honour of the next dance.'

'Wickham, you heard the lady. She does not wish to dance with someone she does not know.' One of the Denton brothers stepped up to Alexandra's side and faced the man, whose name appeared to be Wickham.

'You know the lady?' asked the second man.

'I have had the honour of an *introduction*,' was the cold reply by the gentleman, who, since he claimed to have been introduced, must be Lord Robert.

'Splendid,' exclaimed the inebriated man. 'Since you know us as well, you can introduce us.'

'My Lady, do you wish to be introduced to these... persons?' asked Lord Robert in his most polite manner.

'I would be most happy to be introduced to *gentlemen*,' Alexandra replied with her sweetest smile. 'Since there are none present, whom I have not already been introduced to, I would rather return to my aunt. If you would be so kind as to escort me?' she asked the gentleman at her side.

The second man exclaimed, 'you little...' and tried to grab Alexandra's arm, only to find his wrist held by the second Denton brother, who had been standing unnoticed behind him.

'My dear boy, it is not gentlemanlike to try to grab a lady,' the gentleman purred.

'My Lady,' the first brother said while offering Alexandra his arm with a small bow.

'Thank you, Sir,' she answered politely, taking the proffered arm.

Her escort, with a challenging look at Wickham, led the lady away.

The drunk shook off the restraining hand. 'You are welcome to her, she is too scrawny for my taste anyway,' and walked away trying to regain his composure, while Wickham tried to appear nonchalant as he followed his friend.

When Lady Alexandra and her escort reached the Countess of Marven, her escort's brother caught up with them.

'Thank you for rescuing my niece, Lord Robert.' Lady Beatrice addressed Alexandra's escort. 'Judging by your looks, you must be Lord Denmere.' She smiled at this brother. 'Thank you also for your assistance.'

The first gentleman quickly glanced around and judged that they had privacy. 'Lady Beatrice, I must apologise for a small deception. Would you allow me to introduce my brother, Lord Robert Flinter?'

Lady Beatrice smiled graciously. 'I am delighted to meet you, Sir. Alexandra, I would like you to meet Lord Robert Flinter,' the countess indicated Robert with twinkling eyes, 'and I believe you already know Lord Alistair, the Marquess of Denmere.'

Alexandra curtsied somewhat impertinently and acknowledged the introduction, 'it is my pleasure to finally meet you properly, My Lords.'

The Countess smiled mischievously. 'I must congratulate you on your fortune to have an identical brother. Considering how practised you are, I would guess this is not the first time you both act as each other?'

'Alistair hates being hunted, so I let him use my name when he needs to.' Robert grinned at the ladies, who were amused rather than offended that they had been fooled.

Alexandra laughed at Alistair. 'No wonder you are so familiar with the trials of being prey. But I must add my thanks for your timely rescue. Who were those men?'

'They were Gerald Stone, Viscount Braxton and George Wickham, sycophant of Braxton. Wickham's father is the steward at Pemberley. I presume you know of the Darcy estate in Derbyshire?' Lord Denmere explained.

'I am familiar with the names of Darcy and Braxton,' Lady Beatrice replied. 'To the best of my knowledge, they are the opposites of each other. Mr Wickham I had obviously not heard of, but considering the company he keeps...'

'According to my information, you are correct, My Lady.' Alistair confirmed her unvoiced suspicions. 'Although, I admit I was surprised at how persistent Wickham was. He has a reputation to prefer easy prey.'

'He may have been trying to show off to Braxton,' surmised Robert.

'In that case, I am doubly grateful for your assistance.' Alexandra said. 'To both of you.'

'Any time,' the brothers said in unison. 'It was our pleasure. We enjoy foiling scoundrels and rescuing damsels in distress,' Robert continued.

Alexandra smiled at the brothers. 'Let us make a pact then. Whenever we are in company, we will rescue each other from tedious conversation, fortune-hunters and scoundrels.'

'A pact it is,' agreed Alistair with a grin.

~~H~~

'What did you think of Lord Robert Flinter?' asked Lady Beatrice the following day.

'He is intelligent, charming and good fun,' replied Alexandra.

'And...' prompted her aunt.

'There is no *and*. I hope you are not suggesting I should be looking for a husband already,' Alexandra was horrified.

'He would be an excellent match. His brother will be Duke one day, and he seems to have no problem with being a second son. From what I hear, he is wealthy in his own right, and he seems intelligent as well as good looking. You also seem to like him.'

'Aunt, you promised to give me time. I am only seventeen, and have not even been presented yet,' Alexandra protested. 'I would like a chance to look around before I make a decision...'

'Very well, you shall compare the merchandise on the marriage mart,' Lady Beatrice laughed. 'Although I must warn you, Lord Robert is probably the best match you will ever meet.'

~~H~~

7 London Seasons 1803

1803

The following year, Lady Beatrice, the Countess of Marven was pleased to present Lady Alexandra Hunt to London society.

The beginning of the season coincided with Lady Alex's eighteenth birthday and the end of Lady Beatrice's official guardianship of her niece. Because Lady Beatrice had no other commitments and the two ladies were very fond of each other, she remained in residence with her niece. Since Alexandra needed a companion due to the demands of propriety which claimed that a young woman could not live on her own, the presence of her aunt served a double purpose. It also gave the impression that Alexandra was still under the guardianship of her aunt.

After Alexandra's presentation at court, which had been arranged in a private audience to minimise awareness of her independence, they called on select friends and were invited to attend a variety of soirees, dinners, and balls.

~~H~~

As a counter to all her social engagements, Alexandra loved to go riding early in the morning. Even though she took a groom with her, the man's taciturnity was most welcome, as it allowed her thoughts free rein. Since most members of society slept late, Rotten Row, which was usually crowded at noon, was only sparsely populated in the early hours.

One morning, she had just arrived at Rotten Row, when she spotted a very small rider on a large horse cantering a short distance ahead of her. She was just in time to see an urchin throw something at the pair, which must have hit the horse, as it suddenly reared, before taking off at a frantic gallop, leaving the rider unbalanced and clinging to the saddle.

Without even thinking, Alexandra urged Pegasus after the bolting horse. As she sped along, she was grateful of the smooth sandy surface of the road, and that it was deserted. As she came closer, she saw that the white-faced rider was a young boy.

Alexandra manoeuvred Pegasus closer to the sweating horse. When she was within range, she leaned over and managed to get hold of the reins, which the boy had dropped. When she gently pulled, the horse which was starting to calm down after its fright, responded by slowing down. By the time they reached the end of the road, the horse was willing to stop.

Keeping hold of both sets of reins, she patted both horses. Pegasus accepted the pats as his due, tossing his head and snorting gently. The other horse was still a little skittish, preventing his rider from calming down.

'I hope that you do not mind my saying so, but I believe it would be advisable if you picked a mount closer to your own size,' she commented with an encouraging grin. 'Although I suppose you would have done well enough, if that urchin had not spooked your horse.'

'Thank you, my lady,' the boy at last found his voice. 'Usually, Hermes is much better behaved. I did not expect him to suddenly take off like that.'

'Do you often ride Hermes?' Alexandra asked curiously.

The boy blushed. 'Ah... no... ah... this is the first time,' he blurted out.

'Why do I get the impression that this was an unauthorised outing?'

The boy hung his head and whispered. 'I was tired of having to ride my pony.'

'So, you had to try the biggest stallion in your father's stable.' Alexandra laughed. 'I can understand the temptation but recommend that you work your way up to it.'

'All would have been well, if he had not been spooked,' the boy now raised his head and defiantly defended his action.

'True, but you cannot count on everything going well. You therefore need to be able to control your mount, even in difficult circumstances.'

Alexandra turned to the groom, who had accompanied her, and had just caught up with them. 'Larkin, would you please check that the young man's horse has not come to any harm from his adventure.'

Larkin dismounted and exchanged his reins with that of Hermes. As he led the horse a few steps, he noticed a slight limp. 'I think it would be best if the young master dismounted, to minimise the strain.'

The boy looked crestfallen. 'My father will kill me,' he mourned as he dismounted.

'Who is your father?'

'William Molyneux, the Earl of Sefton,' the boy responded, still worrying about his father's reaction to his favourite stallion being injured.

'And that would make you...'

'Charles William Molyneux, Viscount Molyneux, at your service.' The young Viscount remembered his manners. 'May I know your name, my lady?'

'I am Lady Alexandra Hunt, the Countess of Herne. It is a pleasure to make your acquaintance, My Lord.'

'I am honoured to meet you, My Lady.' He bowed. Charles looked embarrassed as he requested. 'Countess, is it asking too much, if I request that you accompany me home. Perhaps hearing that Hermes was injured due to an urchin, might mitigate my father's... ah... displeasure.'

'Where do you live?'

'Our house is in Arlington Street.'

'Very well, I shall come along and explain in glowing detail the nefarious actions of that urchin.' Alexandra grinned at the look of relief on the face of the young viscount. 'Larkin, would you assist his lordship to mount behind me. Then you can lead Hermes.'

Once they were on their way, Charles noticed something. 'You are riding astride,' he exclaimed. 'I thought that ladies only rode side-saddle.'

'You cannot gallop when you are perched in such an insecure position. I have a strong preference for not breaking my neck, just to satisfy conventions.'

The young Viscount sighed. 'I am most grateful that you do not follow conventions, and I must thank you for your aid.'

'You are welcome. But tell me, how old are you?'

'I am seven years of age,' Charles drew himself up to his full height, trying to look impressive.

'You are?'

'Well, almost,' he admitted, as his shoulders slumped a little.

They chatted pleasantly, while they rode at a slow walk, until they arrived at the house in Arlington Street.

~~H~~

As soon as Charles slid off Pegasus' back, the front door opened and a man in his early forties exited the house. 'Charles, where have you been? And why is Hermes being led?'

Alexandra dismounted and greeted the gentleman, 'good morning. Lord Sefton, I presume?'

Charles, desirous of averting his father's displeasure as long as possible, spoke up. 'Father, this lady is Lady Alexandra Hunt, the Countess of Herne. Lady Alexandra, may I introduce my father, Lord William Molyneux, the Earl of Sefton.'

After their greetings, Alexandra suggested, 'there has been a small accident, and Hermes could do with some attention. He has suffered a small strain, after being pelted with a stone by an urchin, and taking off in fright. I must congratulate Lord Molyneux for being able to stay mounted during this episode. Many a lesser rider would have been thrown. Since I was in the vicinity, I was able to offer my assistance by escorting them home.'

Lord Sefton looked a little dubious, at her carefully edited retelling of the event, but decided to accept it for the nonce. 'I am grateful for your assistance to my family, Lady Alexandra. Might I offer you refreshments and introduce you to my wife?'

'I would be delighted to meet Lady Sefton. I have heard many complimentary things about her.'

Lord Sefton offered her his arm, as he told his son, 'off to the schoolroom with you, young man. We will discuss this later.'

Charles was only too happy to escape his father's potential ire for the moment, and followed the instructions, after expressing his thanks once more to Lady Alexandra, and noting that staff had arrived to take the horses to the stables.

~~H~~

Lord Sefton led Alexandra to the morning room, where Lady Sefton was pacing. The gentleman introduced the ladies and gave his wife the gist of what had occurred.

'I must thank you for bringing our son home, Lady Alexandra. I was most concerned when I discovered that Charles had snuck out with Hermes. That boy is simply smitten with horses.'

Her husband gave an indulgent chuckle. 'He comes by his passion honestly. I too cannot resist a good horse.' Once their guest was settled with a cup of tea, Lord Sefton asked, 'what did really happen to Charles? While the story you recounted sounded quite plausible, I suspect that there is more to the story.'

'Everything I told you is what happened,' Alexandra prevaricated.

Lord Sefton still looked unconvinced. 'Please, Lady Alexandra, tell me all. Do not be concerned that Charles will suffer unduly, since Hermes' injuries are only slight.'

'Very well since you insist and will not punish him excessively. When Hermes reared, he dropped the reins, and during that frantic gallop, he was unable to reclaim them. Fortunately, Pegasus lived up to his name and I was able to catch up with Hermes and bring him to a stop. But as I said before, Lord Molyneux did well not to be thrown.'

Lord Sefton shook his head in mock despair. 'Although it seems too much like rewarding him for his unauthorised ride and endangering himself and my horse, I suppose I had better get him a horse to replace his pony.'

'It might be best. That way he will not be tempted to embark on excursions on his own.'

Now that the events of the morning had been settled, Lady Sefton commented, 'I have heard of your presentation at court, and was hoping to meet you. It is highly unusual for a woman to inherit a title. All London is abuzz with the news.'

Alexandra looked somewhat chagrined as she said, 'I could almost wish that I had a brother, then I would not have to deal with all that bother.'

'You do not like being a countess?'

'Please, do not misunderstand, I like it well enough, but I dislike being treated as a curiosity, like some kind of a five-day wonder.'

Lady Sefton laughed. 'Do not trouble yourself too much. Even though you are a nine-day wonder, after ten days the novelty will wear off for the members of the *ton*. Then someone else, or a new scandal will replace their interest in you.'

The two ladies continued their chat, and even though Lady Sefton was about a dozen years her senior, Alexandra found her remarkably easy to talk to. But soon she recalled herself to the time and took her leave.

Lady Sefton promised to call on Alexandra very soon.

~~H~~

A few days later, Lady Beatrice was pleased to welcome Lady Sefton, who came to call in company of a few of her friends. Those friends just happened to be the patronesses of Almack's.

At the end of the call, Lady Beatrice was even more pleased. With a personal invitation by those ladies to attend a ball at Almack's, Alexandra could no longer demur visiting that institution.

~~H~~

Lady Alexandra attended various events with mixed feelings. Like many young ladies, she enjoyed the company of interesting people, good conversation and she loved to dance. This enjoyment was tempered with the warnings of her guardian and her good friends that most young men would be more interested in her wealth and position than in her as a person.

Her aunt even provided her with a list of gentlemen, detailing their background and information about their character. There were warnings against any number of names, such as gambler, rake, drunkard, spendthrift and some even claimed a vicious temper.

She found out that she had been spoiled by the company she had enjoyed most of her life. The gentlemen who paid attention to her made her doubt the fitness of the human race, and it made her curious about her aunt's sources of, apparently very accurate, information.

Some of the gentlemen and conversations stood out in her mind.

~~H~~

'Young woman,' wheezed the Viscount of ---. 'How dare you style yourself as Countess of Herne. Countess is a courtesy title reserved for the wife of an Earl, not the unmarried daughter of one. You shame your family by putting on airs.'

'My Lord, you are obviously not as well informed as you ought to be,' Alexandra gritted her teeth at the old bore's ranting, who had been trying to put her in her place for the last ten minutes. She suspected that his main problem was the fact that her own rank was higher than his. 'As the heir to my deceased father, I am the Countess of Herne suo jure.'

'Women cannot hold titles in their own right,' the old Viscount insisted. 'That is against nature.'

'It is surprising you never heard of Henrietta Godolphin, the second Duchess of Marlborough, who still lived when you were born. And, I believe, she was almost a neighbour to you.' Alexandra added her parting shot with a raised eyebrow, while the Viscount still spluttered behind her.

~~H~~

Then there was Randolph Stone, the nephew of her great-aunt Felicity, who insisted on pestering Alexandra on the strength of family connections, no matter how tenuous they might be.

'Cousin Alexandra, when I am the Earl, you will not have to worry your pretty little head about business. I am certain it will not be long before I will have everything back to running properly.'

'Cousin Randolph, pray tell, why do you think that Herne Hyde is not running as it should be?' she asked in a deceptively pleasant tone.

'My dear cousin, an estate never runs properly without a Master overseeing it. Your steward may be excellent, but there are decisions only the master of an estate can and should make. I am convinced your steward does his best, but an estate needs a Master.'

'My estate has a Master,' corrected Lady Alexandra. When Randolph looked puzzled, she added, 'I am the Master.'

He smiled patronisingly. 'I am certain you are a wonderful Mistress of Herne Hyde, but no woman can be Master. Their minds are not capable of dealing with the intricacies of business.'

'How could you possibly know how to run an estate, since you have never done so.'

'Uncle Durham has done me the honour of instructing me on estate management and has been instrumental in my training.'

'Oh dear, that does not bode well for your future. From reports which I have had, great-uncle Durham has yet to learn that an estate is supposed to be managed in such a way that it is profitable. Running it further and further into debt, is generally frowned upon.'

Randolph blanched. Uncle Durham must not be aware that Lady Alexandra was very well informed about the state of his finances. Durham had sponsored his nephew for the season, in the expectation that Randolph would be able to secure Alexandra, whom he expected to be an inexperienced young girl; and more importantly her wealth, which Randolph would share with his uncle.

He received a further shock when Alexandra continued. 'You also labour under another misconception. I already pointed this out to Aunt Durham more than a year ago. I am the Countess of Herne, but the man I marry will never be the Earl. That title will eventually go to my oldest son.' Alexandra smiled sweetly. 'No mere male will ever be able to usurp my position.'

She had the satisfaction of seeing stunned disbelief and chagrin on her cousin's face before she turned her back on him and walked away.

~~H~~

Mr Newton was not interested in her title, only her wealth.

'Why do you concern yourself with such menial tasks as running an estate. That is why you hire a steward. You should stay in town and enjoy everything that society has to offer,' Mr Newton suggested.

'Because unlike you, I do not enjoy drinking to excess and suffer the aftereffects, which will eventually give you jaundice. I also have no interest in gambling. I prefer to use my money for more appealing pursuits. I am fully aware that you need a bride to cover your gambling debts with her dowry. I should warn you, that ploy only works once.'

The gentleman gaped at her. 'How...' he spluttered.

'Are you asking how do I know about these things or how do I know these things *about you*?' Lady Alexandra asked sweetly. 'You should know that my guardians have made enquiries about all potential suitors. You may wish to spread the word amongst your friends, wastrels need not apply.'

~~H~~

'How did you get on with Cousin Randolph last night?' asked Lady Beatrice at breakfast the next day.

'Would you believe he tried to convince me that he could run the estate better than I can.' Alexandra chuckled. 'Do not worry your pretty little head about it. Women are incapable of understanding the intricacies of business,' she mimicked her cousin's tone.

'I presume you disabused him of that notion?'

'Naturally. I also disabused him of the notion that my husband would be the Earl. He was not happy about either of my arguments.'

'Mr Newton wanted to show me the delights of town living, and I cannot remember all the other inane topics of conversation.' Alexandra sighed, 'you were correct once again, most men are only interested in me for my money and of course as a broodmare.'

~~H~~

8 Return to the country

Alexandra was grateful when she could return to Herne Hyde. Even though she had not had any great expectations of meeting a potential future husband, witnessing the frenetic hunt for a match by so many young, or even not so young, people, had been unpalatable. Especially since many did not seem to care about compatibility and were only interested in increasing their fortunes.

Admittedly, it had not been all bad, but her rank put her in an awkward position. She had met several pleasant gentlemen, but they had been put off by her circumstances. Most men were not prepared to take a subordinate role to their wife. And to make matters worse for them, they would not even have access to Alexandra's fortune.

The Viscount of Harrington had seemed interested and interesting, but his estate was in Northumberland, while Herne Hyde was in Gloucestershire. The distance between the estates was simply too great, to come to a workable solution.

'I am glad that Aunt Beatrice suggested that I should take my time choosing a husband,' Alexandra told her sister, the evening after her return, when the two girls chatted privately before going to bed.

'The Viscount is a very pleasant man, and if I were in a different position, I might have been tempted to encourage him. But while I like him well enough, I cannot see myself spending the rest of my life with him. There was something missing.'

'You do not love him? Is that really so important?'

'Do you remember our parents? The way they acted towards each other?'

'I remember that they were happy to spend time together.' Daphne considered the implication of her memories. 'I never really thought about it before, but I always assumed that all married couples were like that.'

'Indeed not. I have seen a number of couples who can barely stand being in the same room. Or, at best, be indifferent towards their spouse.'

'You want a husband whom you can love.' Daphne stated, rather than asked.

'That and respect.' Alexandra agreed with a sigh.

Daphne grimaced. 'Based on what you have told me about the men you met, all I can say is, good luck. You will need it.'

~~H~~

For Alexandra, the highlight of the season had been her meeting with Lord Molyneux, and she delighted in relating the episode to her sister and to Amelia.

'That boy is lucky to have understanding parents,' commented Daphne.

'I suppose we are even luckier,' suggested Amelia with a shy smile. She still had trouble believing in her good fortune. She was old enough to realise that she and Daphne were unusual, but even more extraordinary was the fact that her own family, and Daphne's family, were prepared to encourage them, rather than insist that they conform to society's conventions and expectations.

'You mean because it is acceptable for a boy to be adventurous, but for girls to be intelligent is frowned upon.'

'Precisely. Remember the story I told you about that time mother took me to a bookshop, and I heard a woman berate her daughter about being too bookish and too much of a hoyden, and for that reason she would never get a husband. The girl could not have been much above ten years of age. Why would her mother worry about her getting married at that age?'

Lady Beatrice, who had listened to the conversation, suggested, 'because most girls do not have a choice, but to get married. There are very few options for women to earn a respectable living. Also, many men dislike bluestockings. They look down upon and denigrate them. I suspect that they do so because they feel threatened by intelligent women. Therefore, they try to prevent these women from receiving an education, using spacious arguments about women being incapable of learning.'

'Of course, women are incapable of becoming educated... since the men prevent them from getting an education,' huffed Daphne. 'In other words, kill the threat, before it can become a threat. Very convenient.'

'Daphne, do not allow yourself to get embittered by these injustices. There are some men who like intelligent, independent, and forceful women. But while they are in the minority, we have to learn to deal with society as it is,' Lady Beatrice tried to calm her niece.

Daphne looked rebellious at that statement, until Alexandra reminded her, 'at least no one will ever force you into a marriage, and you will be able to live your life how you want to. If you happen to meet a man you wish to marry, that is your choice. If you wish to remain single, that is perfectly acceptable as well.'

Amelia grinned. 'Daphne, just think. The two of us could share a house and spend our life researching anything that takes our fancy. I believe you could not wish for better.'

Daphne returned the smile and exclaimed, 'very well. We shall become two eccentric old ladies together. But instead of keeping cats, we shall keep a laboratory.'

~~H~~

Alexandra, having spent three months in London, and only been able to confer with her stewards via correspondence, threw herself into the business of managing her estates with enthusiasm.

Farmers and crops and even animals were much more predictable than the people she had met in Town. Or, at least, she was able to understand them more easily. They generally did not have any hidden agendas.

Taking Pegasus out to inspect the estates was a pleasure, giving her time and the opportunity to consider the events in town. Her aunt had tried to prepare her for the reception she would receive by the members of society, but the reality of many of the reactions was still disappointing.

She felt lonely. Being in charge of her own fate, set her apart from others. Aunt Beatrice was a wonderful woman, and a great support, but something was still lacking.

Alexandra realised that she had wealth and position, but she did not have friends. At least not the kind of friends with whom she could discuss whatever troubled her. An equal, who would understand her, and not consider her ungrateful because she bemoaned the fact that her position caused her to be an outsider.

She was even a little jealous of her sister, who had such a good friend in Amelia. While Alexandra would never do anything to jeopardise that friendship, she fervently wished for such a relationship for herself.

She hoped that the next time she was in London, she would have the opportunity to meet the Denton Doubles. She had enjoyed the easy camaraderie with them, on the occasion of their one meeting.

~~H~~

The night of the full moon was approaching, heralding the monthly assembly in the village of Huntington, an event which Alexandra enjoyed for several reasons. Many of her neighbours had known her all her life and treated her as a person, rather than as an oddity. It also gave her an opportunity to catch up on the latest events amongst the people whom she saw infrequently.

As usual, Daphne and Amelia refused to attend, with the excuse that they were not officially out in society yet. They dismissed the argument that in their small neighbourhood it was irrelevant if they had made their curtsies to the Queen, or not, and that at the age of sixteen, almost seventeen, it was quite acceptable for them to attend a local function.

Since the two girls would not be moved, Alexandra and her aunt planned to attend the assembly without them.

As they were ready to leave, each lady complimented her companion on their choice of dress. 'Madam Bouchard has outdone herself with your latest gown, Alexandra. This simple and understated elegance suits you extremely well. Just enough lace to soften the outline.'

'You should know, Aunt, since you also chose one of that lady's creations. I must admit, it is a relief that her good taste is being appreciated by the ladies in Town.' Alexandra agreed with her aunt, before she asked, 'I meant to find out earlier, is there likely to be anyone of interest at the assembly tonight?'

'I believe that Mr Harper's niece is visiting for the summer. No one else has houseguests at present.'

'I hope the young lady enjoys her stay. It would be nice to have another young lady, of similar age, around.'

~~H~~

Alexandra stood by the door to the balcony, sipping on a glass of lemonade, enjoying the slightly cooler air coming in through the open doors.

She watched as young Mr Hotchkins escorted Miss Harper to the chairs, set against the wall between the balcony doors. The young woman did not look pleased with her surroundings.

Uncertain if the young lady was put out on being left on her own, or for some other reason, Alexandra decided to speak to her.

'You must be Miss Harper. Allow me to introduce myself. I am Alexandra Hunt, of Herne Hyde.'

'How do you know who I am?' asked Miss Harper in a sulky tone of voice. Apparently, being left on her own was not her problem.

'I saw you arrive with Mr Harper, and since I had heard that his niece was visiting for the summer, I assumed that you must be that niece.'

'I am indeed Miss Arabella Harper.' She examined Alexandra from head to foot, taking in the restrained elegance of the gown, and seemingly found it wanting. 'Pardon me for saying so, but being unfamiliar with country manners, I am all astonishment that you would introduce yourself.'

The young woman looked down her nose at Alexandra, even though, being of similar height, she had to bend her head backwards to do so.

Alexandra suppressed an amused smile and answered politely. 'This is a small community, and we all know one another. As a result, we generally do not stand on much formality, and we try to make newcomers welcome.'

'I suppose it must be quite exciting to have visitors from Town in your midst, presenting you with an opportunity to see fashionable dress and manners in such a rustic neighbourhood.' It seemed that Miss Harper did not only suffer from the sulks, but also from superciliousness.

'It is indeed a source of great delight to us, to observe ladies and gentlemen with exquisite manners and taste.' Alexandra gave a bland smile, not betraying the fact that she thought that Miss Harper was not such a lady. She absently noted that their conversation was attracting the notice of other celebrants.

Miss Harper, from her position of supposed superiority as a lady who usually lived in London suggested, 'perhaps you would benefit from a season in Town, Miss Hunt. I would be delighted to provide you with an introduction to my dressmaker. Then you too could be fashionably attired.' She gave Alexandra's gown a pointed look.

Since the young woman, Alexandra now refused to think of her as a lady, was determined to be contemptuous, Lady Alex could not resist commenting, 'I could not possibly impose on you like that. I am sure that your dressmaker's creations would give my acquaintances a false impression of my status.'

'My dear Miss Hunt, even if you have to save your allowance for several months, every young lady should have at least one dress in which to show off.' With every exchange Miss Harper became more patronising.

Alexandra noticed several people listening to their exchange and frowning at the visitor behind her back. 'I doubt that I could carry off such lace and feathers which adorn your gown. It also requires a particular complexion to wear such a vibrant shade of orange.'

Miss Harper preened. 'It is the most fashionable colour this season,' she declared proudly.

One of their neighbours, Mrs Peebles, pressed a hand against her mouth to contain the snort she had been about to utter. Her friend, Mrs Lorrimer, was not as subtle as she muttered, 'I bet it is.'

Since Alexandra appeared to be an attentive and respectful audience, Miss Harper indicated one of the other ladies in the room. 'Do you see that woman over there? The one in that excessively plain dark blue gown.'

'Yes, I see her.' Alexandra wondered what comments Miss Harper might have in store for Aunt Beatrice.

'She looks like a crow at a funeral. Her dress is so plain that in Town only a tradesman's wife would be caught wearing it. And even they would not wear it to a ball. No feathers, no lace, no contrasting ribbons even. I wonder where she could have gotten such a plain costume?'

'I believe she had it made by Madam Bouchard,' Alexandra responded truthfully, waiting for Miss Harper's reaction with carefully suppressed glee.

'Madam Bouchard?' The young woman asked in confusion.

'Have you not heard of Madame Bouchard? I thought you knowledgeable on matters of fashion.'

'There is a Madam Bouchard in Oxford Street. She is London's premier modiste. But she would never design such a plain gown.'

'You must be very familiar with her designs, to make such a statement. Do you frequent her salon often?'

'Not yet, she has always been too busy, for me to get an appointment,' Miss Harper was forced to concede, before she exclaimed, 'how could that drab woman get an appointment with Madame Bouchard, when the lady did not even have time to see me, to make an appointment?' spluttered Miss Harper.

To her misfortune, she had been too focused on her conversation with Alexandra, to notice the approach of the lady under discussion.

Lady Beatrice smiled at her niece. 'Alexandra my dear, will you introduce me to your new acquaintance?'

'Of course, it will be my pleasure. Aunt Beatrice, this is Miss Arabella Harper, Mr Harper's niece. Miss Harper, I would like to introduce you to my aunt, Lady Beatrice, the Countess of Marven.'

The introduction, delivered with a polite smile, was received in stunned silence by the young woman, who stared at the Countess, and realised that at close quarters, she could see that the shimmering silk of the gown was delicately embroidered with the same dark blue, but matte, thread, interspersed with gold thread. The workmanship was superb and subtle.

'Miss Harper, are you quite well? Pardon me for saying so, but you appear to be quite discomposed,' Lady Beatrice enquired solicitously.

Mrs Peebles, commented sotto voce, 'I think a cat got her tongue.'

Mrs Lorrimer suggested, 'I think not. I think the cat wished she never had a tongue.'

Their musings were interrupted by Mr Harper, who arrived with a cup of punch for his niece.

'My dear Arabella, I see that you have met the two leading ladies of our community.' He handed the cup to his niece and bowed to the ladies. 'Lady Beatrice, it is good to see you again. I hope that you have been well?' Once Lady Beatrice assured him of her good health, he addressed Alexandra. 'Lady Alexandra, I am most grateful to you to entertain my niece while I was unavoidably delayed.'

'Think nothing of it, Mr Harper. I found my conversation with Miss Harper quite instructive.'

Miss Harper, who had taken a big gulp from her cup after discovering the identity of Lady Beatrice, now croaked, 'Lady Alexandra?'

Mr Harper smiled at her. 'Arabella, you are indeed fortunate to be in company with the Countess of Herne.' The gentleman transferred his smile to the lady he named.

Miss Harper looked at Alexandra in consternation, wishing the ground would open up and swallow her. Since the ground refused to cooperate, she quickly drained the rest of the punch, pressed the cup into her uncle's hands and rushed out of the hall.

Mr Harper appeared confused at his niece's reaction. 'What did I say?' he enquired of no one in particular.

~~H~~

9 *London Seasons 1804*

In her second season, Alexandra again met Frederick, the Earl of Marven. By that time, he had sold everything he could, to cover his debts and was now desperate to find a wife. Any wife. He needed a well-endowed woman, based on finance, not physical attributes.

When he had no luck in the circles which he usually frequented, he decided to try for his cousin, who, due to her tender age, should be unable to resist him – one way or another.

He thought that luck was in his favour at last when he encountered Lady Alexandra at a ball without her aunt in attendance. Apparently, Lady Beatrice was feeling unwell and had deputised her companion, Mrs Hodges, to chaperone her niece.

Events did not unfold how he had envisaged.

'No, Cousin Frederick, I have no interest in the view from the balcony,' Alexandra said firmly.

When he ignored her protest and tried to pull her to the balcony by her arm, she said, 'I repeat, I have no interest in the view from the balcony and if you do not unhand me this instant, I will remove your hand.'

'Come now, Cousin, do not make a scene,' Frederick said while trying to drag Alexandra towards the balcony.

Lady Alexandra said with a saccharine smile, 'I am not making a *scene*, I am making an example.' Then she moved in ways unexpected by the Earl.

'F*#@'

'Is there a doctor in the house?' asked Alexandra. 'It appears my cousin has injured his wrist.'

~~H~~

'Congratulations, I have wanted to do that for years,' said a quiet voice in Lady Alexandra's ear after Frederick had been helped out of the room by two servants.

She turned around to look at the speaker. She saw a young man of about five and twenty, of medium height and build, with light brown hair and grey eyes. He looked at her with admiration and an amused smile.

'I thank you for saving me the trouble of stepping in and making a spectacle of myself. You handled yourself, and the Earl, beautifully. I doubt anyone else noticed. You have no idea what a delight it is, to see a damsel dealing out distress.'

'I do not believe we have been introduced,' Alexandra said cautiously.

'Since your cousin, who could have introduced us, is hors de combat at present, would you allow me to introduce myself?' At Alexandra's nod he bowed and said, 'I am Sir Marcus Scott, Baron of Vintington. At your service.'

'Lady Alexandra Hunt. I am pleased to meet you... I think.' Alexandra curtsied. 'I gather you know my cousin?'

'Will you take it amiss if I say I had the misfortune to meet him?'

'I may not take it amiss if you can tell me the circumstances.'

'It was at a house-party where... I am sorry, I am not certain if I should disclose such a distasteful tale to a lady.' Sir Marcus suddenly seemed to realise who he was speaking with.

'Let me guess. Housemaid?'

'Parlourmaid. I hired her the same day, when I left the house-party because the host fired the girl for having the misfortune to be molested by one of his guests. She is an excellent parlourmaid. My housekeeper was very happy with the addition to her staff.'

'Pray tell, how it came about that you were in company of a man who would not protect his staff?'

'I went to school with my host's younger brother who is decent enough. Unfortunately, he is dependent on his brother. May I ask, how close a cousin is he?'

'He is a cousin of my aunt's late husband.'

'The previous Earl of Marven was your uncle?'

When Alexandra supplied, 'he was my uncle by marriage', he continued. 'I only met him once, but I found him an interesting conversationalist. Some of his ideas were quite singular.'

'I believe he also rescued a parlourmaid or two in his time,' Alexandra smiled, remembering the stories told, by some of the maids her aunt had sent to Herne Hyde after her uncle's death.

'That was what I found interesting about him. A man of rank who felt it was incumbent on him to act like a true gentleman.' Sir Marcus smiled at his own memories. 'May I now be a gentleman and fetch you some refreshments after your exertions?' he offered.

'A glass of hock would be most welcome,' Alexandra requested.

'You prefer a dry wine to a sweet punch?' Sir Marcus said, surprised.

'The punch they serve here packs too much of a punch for me,' she quipped.

'Oh dear. I thought you were perfect. Now I learn that you like bad puns. But you shall have your wish, and I will gird my loins and fight my way through the crowds to retrieve the beverage of your choice.' Marcus smiled as he went on his errand.

Alexandra watched him saunter away. She was bemused. Although Sir Marcus had affected manners, he moved with the smoothness of a fighter. She also noted with appreciation the exquisite fit of his costume, which was elegant, rather than ostentatious, and enhanced a trim figure.

He returned speedily with two glasses of wine. 'It appears that most people prefer the punch. There were no crowds for me to fight.'

'I shall enjoy the wine all the same,' replied Alexandra as she accepted her glass and took a sip.

'Would you care to sit down?' Marcus indicated a small table with two chairs at the side of the room near a window, but in full view of the room. 'I believe it might be a little cooler there.'

Alexandra was happy to agree. This gentleman seemed to have more conversation than the usual run of the mill peers.

'Would you satisfy my curiosity and tell me how you became so proficient in dealing with pests?' Sir Marcus was intrigued by this young lady, who appeared demure despite her ability to deal with unwanted attention.

'Would you believe my father was an expert exterminator?' Alexandra could not resist the tease.

Over the course of the next hour, she found that Sir Marcus could converse on a variety of subjects and apparently enjoyed a lively debate.

That night, after returning to Hunt House with Mrs Hodges, for the first time in her life Alexandra fell asleep while thinking of a pair of warm grey eyes, a mischievous smile, and a wicked sense of humour. Unbeknownst to her, while she slept, a soft smile graced her features.

~~H~~

'How was the ball last night?' asked Lady Beatrice at breakfast the next day. She was recovering from the stomach upset that had plagued her for the last two days.

'It was interesting, to say the least,' Alexandra smirked.

'Anything I should know about?' her aunt was curious.

'Cousin Frederick was at the ball...' Alexandra replied in an off-handed manner to peak her aunt's interest.

'I did not think that the Carstairs would invite him, considering they have two daughters,' Lady Beatrice replied in surprise.

'I think he arrived late, with a group of friends.' Alexandra was still dragging out her story.

'I get the feeling that something happened. Pray tell, what did he do?'

'I believe he was determined to get engaged last night,' Alexandra shrugged carelessly.

'Who did he think would be stupid or desperate enough to want to marry him?' Lady Beatrice chuckled until a thought struck her. 'Wait, you said he was *determined* to get engaged. Are you telling me that he tried to compromise a lady?'

'I suspect that was on his mind when he insisted that I should admire the view from the balcony.'

'He tried to compromise *you*?' Lady Beatrice was aghast. She studied her niece carefully. 'Since you appear quite cheerful, I gather he was unsuccessful?'

'He tried to drag me outside when I refused to go voluntarily, and he was most upset when I injured his wrist,' Alexandra smirked. 'Please remind me to send a letter of thanks to Mr Martin. His instructions were most efficacious.'

'Did anyone notice what happened?' Although Lady Beatrice was pleased that the Earl had been unsuccessful and her niece was safe, she was concerned about potential negative gossip.

'Only one gentleman noticed because he apparently was just getting ready to rescue me. He was most complimentary about the fact that I was no damsel in distress,' replied Alexandra with a slight blush.

Her aunt noticed the blush and became very curious indeed. 'Who was this remarkable gentleman?' she asked.

'He is Sir Marcus Scott, Baron of Vintington. He was not on my list, but I believe he knew your husband.'

'A Baron, hmm? I do not recall your uncle mentioning him at the moment, but he had many acquaintances.' Lady Beatrice was intrigued. 'I am afraid the list I provided to you stopped at Viscounts. It appears we have to extend our criteria,' she mused. 'What was Lord Scott like?'

'He prefers to be addressed as Sir Marcus. He seems intelligent and well-read and appears to enjoy elegant discourse. He has a quirky sense of humour. I would guess he is about five and twenty. While he is not classically handsome, he is pleasing to look at. We did not dance but I noticed that he moves with grace... the grace of a fighter,' Alexandra told her aunt.

Lady Beatrice hid her amusement when she noticed the enthusiasm in Alexandra's demeanour. 'Are you likely to see him again?' she asked.

'Since we both have invitations to the Worthington ball next week, I expect to see him there.'

'He was invited by the Worthington's? That speaks well for him. They are very particular about their guests,' Lady Beatrice said in a thoughtful voice. 'Now tell me more about this Baron who has you so interested on such short an acquaintance.'

'What makes you think I am interested?' Alexandra protested.

'Because for the first time you are saying nice things about a man...'

'I have said nice things about Lord Denmere and Lord Robert,' Alexandra interrupted.

'True, but neither of them made you blush.'

Alexandra raised her hands to her hot cheeks and said, 'Oh...'

~~H~~

Alexandra retired early to give herself the opportunity to consider her aunt's words about Sir Marcus. Although she needed no special time to think about the gentleman since he had never been far from her mind all day.

Her aunt had said that speaking about Sir Marcus had made her blush.

She admitted to herself that she had found his company enjoyable. He had treated her with respect and listened to her opinions, even when he disagreed with them. Or appeared to disagree with them. She suspected that he had voiced opinions that were not his own, to see whether she would try to refute them.

Was that because he liked women who had opinions of their own or was he trying to find out if she was prepared to argue with him, to avoid her in the future. Because he, like other men, wanted a woman who would always be agreeable and subservient.

On further consideration, she did not think he was offended by her speaking her mind. Had he not congratulated her on her handling of Cousin Frederick?

Apart from his conversation, she also liked his looks. Although Sir Marcus was not as tall as some men, only a few inches taller than she was, the way he moved lent him a stature that most other men seemed to lack.

He moved with a purpose which seemed to be missing in most other young men of her acquaintance. She supposed that having the responsibility of managing an estate thrust upon him unexpectedly at an early age, had matured him.

When he had first addressed her, she had immediately noticed warm grey eyes, full of humour and, she thought, admiration. Later, as he handed her the glass of wine that he had fetched for her, she saw that his hands were well shaped and cared for. Although he had calluses which indicated he handled more than just eating utensils.

Overall, he cut a fine figure in his elegant, but understated, clothes.

She realised with chagrin that for a man, whom she had only known for an hour, she had noticed a great deal about him.

And that tingly feeling, even through the gloves she had worn, where he kissed her hand, when they said farewell, was a new experience for her. On top of that, what was that fluttery feeling in her stomach every time she thought of him? Could it be...

~~H~~

The self-same gentleman was musing about the young lady he had met the previous evening.

When he had noticed the Earl of Marven trying to manhandle the young lady towards the balcony, Sir Marcus was outraged. He had a passing acquaintance with the man and knew him to be a rake and heavily in debt. He assumed that since the young lady did not seem to be willing to accompany the Earl, Marven was trying to compromise the girl to force her into a, for him, advantageous marriage.

Marcus had started to move in their direction to interfere in Marven's plans, when the young woman seemingly flicked a fly off her wrist and moments later was calling for a doctor, while Marven was holding his injured wrist.

Although he abhorred violence, especially against women and children, he was quite prepared to use it, if circumstances forced his hand. His father had been a great believer in the scholar warrior model for a gentleman's education and Marcus found that the role suited him.

Marcus did not even have to think about it, he had to meet this remarkable lady. Against all propriety, he had addressed her, and she had allowed him to introduce himself.

She seemed cautiously amused by his compliments.

He had been so surprised that she was related to that rake, that, when she enquired about his acquaintance with Marven, he started to tell her about his brief acquaintance with the man, without considering the propriety of the tale. Fortunately, he caught himself before he went too far. It would not do to shock a sheltered young Lady with such a sordid tale.

He was the one to receive a shock when she suggested "housemaid".

The simple statement raised her and her parents in his estimation. Even though she looked perfectly demure, her parents had obviously done her the favour to educate her about the dangers some men presented to women.

He was pleased to note that she was concerned about the welfare of the maid, rather than dismissive, as many Ladies would have been about a servant.

When she accepted his offer of refreshment and had requested a glass of hock rather than sweet punch, he had nearly floated to the refreshment table. Despite the fact that he had complained about her pun, he had been amused by her wit.

The following hour spent in conversation had been the highlight of not only the ball but his entire visit to London.

In retrospect he realised that she was exceedingly attractive. He had noticed that initially when he saw her with Marven. Once they started to speak, her personality had eclipsed her looks until he forgot that she was a lovely lady physically as well as mentally.

She was moderately tall. Only about three inches shorter than himself. She had shiny auburn hair and sparkling hazel eyes. Her figure was slim, and, although delightfully rounded in all the right places, appeared to be quite trim. Unlike some of those flabby debutants he had met recently.

She had been a little reticent about her background. Considering she had called herself Lady Alexandra, she must be the daughter of at least an Earl. That was a little off-putting because he did not wish to appear to be a fortune-hunter, which he was not. Although he was not in the same league financially as some Earls or Dukes, he was very comfortably situated indeed.

At the same time, if she was the daughter of an Earl, her rank was not that much greater, so that he might have a chance. Particularly if she had older sisters. She had not mentioned any sisters, but she might have one or more.

He caught himself when he realised the trend of his thoughts. *For goodness' sake, Marcus*, he chided himself, *get a grip. You have only known her for an hour. It is much too early to even consider the future. After all, she might not even like you…*

~~H~~

10 Worthington Ball

Lady Beatrice was in her element. It was a delight to catch up with old friends. Since it was Alexandra's second season, she was already acquainted with their hosts and did not need an introduction.

Lady Cordelia Worthington was pleased to see Alexandra again. 'How delightful that you could make it to our ball, my dear. We have invited some interesting young men, whose company and conversation you might enjoy. I hope you find their discourse agreeable.'

'You are most considerate, Lady Cordelia. I am exceedingly flattered that you invited me,' Alexandra answered honestly. She had met the lady on a number of occasions and appreciated her company. Her hostess was a lovely and sensible woman who at times delighted to pretend to be scatterbrained. Only her closest friends knew better than to believe the façade she presented to society.

They chatted amiably for another minute or two until the next guests arrived, whereupon Lady Beatrice led Lady Alex into the ballroom. A number of guests were already assembled when they made their entrance.

One gentleman, who had arrived early to ensure he would be able to request the supper dance from Lady Alexandra, was watching for her arrival. He was pleased to note that when her eyes swept the room, they connected with his own. He was even more encouraged when she smiled as she recognised him.

He approached the ladies and bowed to Lady Alexandra. 'My Lady, it is a delight to see you again. I trust you have been well?'

'Good evening, Sir Marcus, I am well and pleased to renew our acquaintance. Thank you for asking,' Alexandra responded to his open smile before turning to her companion to perform the introduction. 'Aunt Beatrice, I would like you to meet Lord Sir Marcus Scott, Baron of Vintington. Sir Marcus, this is my aunt, the Countess of Marven.'

'I am pleased to make your acquaintance, Sir Marcus. I heard many good things about you from my late husband.'

'I am delighted to meet you at last, My Lady. Your niece has spoken much about her wonderful guardian. But I am flattered that your husband mentioned our brief acquaintance to you, and even more so that you would remember such a trifling episode.'

'It was no trifling matter to my husband or to myself that a gentleman would be concerned with the safety of someone else's staff,' Lady Beatrice replied, pleased with her first impression of the young man. 'But I am certain you are not here to discuss old times,' she smiled and nodded at the queue forming behind Sir Marcus.

'Although I would be delighted to discuss anything your heart desires, I admit that I had hoped to request the supper set of your beautiful niece,' Sir Marcus smiled at the older Lady before turning to her niece. 'Please tell me that you have that set available and that you would honour me with those dances, Lady Alexandra.'

'The answer is yes to both,' Alexandra agreed with a smile. 'I shall look forward to dancing with you and having your company for supper.'

'Thank you, My Lady. I shall be the envy of all the gentlemen to have the opportunity for elegant discourse.' Sir Marcus bowed to the ladies and reluctantly made way for the other gentlemen who had come to request dances from Lady Alexandra.

Soon Alexandra's dance card was full, and she had to disappoint several of the gentlemen.

~~H~~

To Alexandra's delight, Lady Cordelia had indeed invited several interesting gentlemen. Although none of these intrigued her as much as Sir Marcus, she had an enjoyable time not discussing the weather.

While they were waiting for the music to start, Lord Bassington asked politely, 'Lady Alexandra, are there any topics you particularly enjoy?'

Alexandra was surprised by the directness of the question, but happily replied, 'I am happy to discuss many things as long as they do not include the weather or the latest fashions.'

That quip caused Lord Bassington to chuckle, 'I admit, the only time I am interested in the weather is when it affects our tenants' ability to grow their produce.'

'I agree, flooded fields can be a problem. We had to improve our drainage system last year or our wheat-fields would have been washed away. We did not wish to risk being unable to deliver the supplies to the army. It would not do, to give Mr Bonaparte any advantages.'

Now it was Lord Bassington's turn to be surprised. 'You are interested in logistics?'

'I am interested in many things which are not usually considered to be in the purview of young ladies,' replied Alexandra.

That comment opened the floodgates for the gentleman. While he could converse on the latest fashions or the on dit, he had no true interest in those subjects. When he discovered his current dance partner had similar disinterests, he thoroughly enjoyed the conversation as well as the dance.

Alexandra's dance partner for the next set was Mr Fitzwilliam Darcy, a young man who appeared to be about her own age or perhaps a year older, and who seemed rather tongue tied at the start.

Alexandra decided that it might be helpful for both their sakes to follow the example of Lord Bassington, she therefore suggested, 'Mr Darcy, would it help you if I mentioned that I enjoy conversing about books, travel, politics and philosophy. Maybe even some history?'

Mr Darcy looked startled and blushed furiously, but answered with a relieved smile, 'that is indeed extremely helpful, My Lady. Personally, I have always preferred reading the plays of Mr Shakespeare rather than watching them in the theatre. In this fashion I can imagine the characters as I wish them to be, rather than being confined by the interpretation of the actors.'

Delighted that she had managed to break the ice with Mr Darcy, Alexandra spent the rest of the set in animated discussion of the relative merits of Mr Shakespeare's comedies versus his tragedies.

~~H~~

At last, the supper set commenced, and Sir Marcus arrived to escort Alexandra to the dancefloor.

Sir Marcus complimented Lady Alexandra. 'You have made quite a conquest tonight. I have never before seen Fitzwilliam Darcy so animated.'

Alexandra laughed. 'All I did was to suggest some topics of conversation which appeal to me, which excluded the weather, ladies' fashion and malicious gossip.'

'This might seem a simple thing to you, but I happen to know that Mr Darcy often finds it difficult to speak to ladies. Which made your suggestions invaluable to him.'

'I am most pleased that I was of assistance. Once he started to speak, he was a delightful conversationalist.' Alexandra was pleased to have been helpful. 'Now, what about you, Sir. Do you wish me to give you a list of topics of conversation to choose from, or do you already have a topic in mind?'

'We had absolutely splendid weather today, did we not?' Sir Marcus suggested cheekily. When Alexandra glowered at him, he laughed. 'I read in the paper today about a discussion in the House of Lords...'

Lady Alexandra and her partner had an enjoyable half an hour dancing and discussing politics.

When supper was announced, Marcus offered Alexandra his arm and escorted her to a table. After asking her preferences he fixed plates for both of them and joined her for more conversation.

They had been chatting for a few minutes when Sir Marcus recalled a conversation from the previous evening. 'Unless you are even more exceptional than I thought, my friend, Lord Robert Flinter, was very confused last night. I believe he was a little under the weather when he called you "the contrary Countess",' Sir Marcus teased his companion.

Alexandra's face lit up. 'Lord Robert? I have not had the pleasure of his company in an age. Is he well? Other than being under the weather, of course.' Alexandra was pleased to hear that this pleasant young man had the good taste to be friends with Robert Flinter.

'He appeared in good health but was disappointed that he would miss tonight's ball. He had been invited but could not accept since, as a new lieutenant in the army, he had to join his unit this morning,' explained Marcus.

'That is most inconsiderate of his superiors. I would have enjoyed seeing him again. It has been too long since we had a chance to visit.'

'Do you know him well?' Marcus was curious.

'I met him and his brother in Cambridge the year before last.' Alexandra chuckled at the memory. 'We made a pact to rescue each other from fortune hunters and tedious conversations. Although, I am happy to say, today I do not need rescuing.'

'Considering what I saw at our last meeting, I do not believe you ever need a gentleman to rescue you,' Sir Marcus complimented her. She had admitted that her instruction in self-defence had come from their butler, rather than her father the "expert exterminator". Marcus felt that all women should be allowed to learn such skills to ensure they would be treated with respect rather than as chattel.

'Only from conversations about the weather,' Alexandra smiled impishly. 'You are a remarkably able rescuer.'

'Thank you for your vote of confidence, My Lady. I must admit that you are also a very capable guardian of my sanity. I wish I had had you to converse with the one time I attended Almack's.'

'I also attended only once, last year. But I could not bear the atmosphere of almost frenetic pursuit.' Alexandra shuddered.

'I detest the marriage mart,' she continued. 'Partners are chosen by how suitable they are financially and social rank. Very little, if any, consideration is given to how suitable the couple are. It is worse for ladies than it is for gentlemen. If a man is poor, or relatively so, he can still earn a living without the social stigma which makes women considered to be unmarriageable because they have held a position.'

'Society is not fair, I agree. I admit that I am grateful that I have no family to dictate how I must marry. What about you? Will your father allow you a choice? Or will he negotiate a marriage for you and present you with a fait accompli?'

'The head of my family will choose my husband,' replied Alexandra evasively. She was curious that Sir Marcus was asking such a specific question on such short an acquaintance.

'I hope for your sake that your father will at least consider your preferences,' Marcus was concerned that such a vibrant young woman could be shackled to some indifferent old nobleman, purely for financial or political gain to the family. Or worse, to the dissolute son of such a nobleman.

'My father passed away four years ago. He will not be making the choice,' Alexandra admitted, but still drawing out the time to admit her real situation.

'Your brother then?' Sir Marcus continued his questions. For some unfathomable reason he could not stop himself, he needed to know who would determine the lady's future.

Alexandra sighed, 'I have no brother.'

'A cousin or uncle then?'

'No cousin and no uncle, and I have to point out that you are exceedingly persistent.'

'I always like to understand, and yet I do not understand your situation,' Sir Marcus was puzzled. 'You said your father was the Earl of Herne. Which means he was the head of your family. Am I correct?'

'That is the case.'

'Since you said your father has passed away, who inherited the title and became the head of your family?' the gentleman still persisted.

Alexandra gave up her prevarication. 'I did,' was the simple answer.

'You did what?'

'I inherited the title and at the termination of my aunt's guardianship, I am the head of the family. It is a very small family of two. Three, if you count my aunt, although she has very independent means.' Alexandra shrugged and smiled self-deprecatingly. 'That is why Lord Robert calls me the contrary countess.'

Sir Marcus was stunned and dismayed. While he thought the enchanting lady was the daughter of an Earl, their stations in society were not so far apart that he might be considered an eligible match for her. But as a Countess in her own right... She could never marry a lowly Baron. She would be expected to marry a man of similar rank to her own.

Damn. Why could she not have a brother. Why was the one woman, whose conversation and company he enjoyed, so far out of his reach. He knew the law well enough to know that her husband would not share in her title. She would probably be best advised to choose the second son of an Earl or a Duke...

That thought gave him pause. Of course, he was a fool. She was friends with Robert Flinter. As the second son of a Duke, he was perfect for her. He took a deep breath to steady himself. Very well, she was out of his reach, but he could still be friends with her and enjoy her conversation.

'In that case, Countess, I hope you make a choice that pleases you.' She appeared not to have noticed the delay in his reply.

'My Aunt, Lady Beatrice, advised me to take my time to find the right partner.' She smiled a little sadly. 'I might rail against society's expectations and restrictions of women. But it is for others of my sex that I am dismayed. I am in the enviable position to have enough rank, wealth and independence to make my own choices without being dictated to by some more or less well-meaning male.'

Marcus chuckled, 'and you have enough skill to enforce your refusal.'

'Will you always remind me of that unladylike behaviour?' Alexandra mourned. 'Truly, I only use it in the most dire of circumstances. But society would consider me terribly risqué if it became common knowledge.'

'I beg your pardon. I had not meant to distress you, but only tried, apparently clumsily, to compliment you,' Sir Marcus reassured her.

'I accept your apology.' Alexandra now decided to change the subject. 'Last week, you complained that I like puns. I must tell you that I come by this trait honestly since it runs in my family.'

When Marcus looked intrigued, she explained, 'when he was granted the earldom, my ancestor was allowed to choose a name for it. Since our family name is Hunt, he chose Herne. I assume you have a classical education?'

'Herne the Hunter. Oh dear,' Sir Marcus chuckled. 'I grant that I cannot blame you for a family trait.'

Having overcome their awkwardness of Lady Alexandra's confession, they returned to their pleasant conversation with renewed enthusiasm.

~~H~~

11 *Meetings*

The following morning, as was their custom, Lady Beatrice and Lady Alex reviewed their evening.

'You seemed to enjoy yourself last night,' commented Lady Beatrice.

'I did, thank you. For once the company was interesting,' replied Lady Alexandra.

'Did anyone in particular interest you?'

'Mr Darcy and Lord Bassington were interesting and pleasant conversationalists.'

'What about Sir Marcus. I noticed you had a most animated conversation with him during supper.'

Alexandra blushed. 'I did indeed have an elegant discourse with the gentleman.'

'Y-e-s...' prompted her aunt.

'I would enjoy speaking to him again,' admitted Alexandra.

'Go on...'

'He appears intelligent, well-educated and has a remarkably liberal attitude towards women's accomplishments. Would you believe he actually complimented me on my handling of Cousin Frederick? Most men would have been horrified that I deliberately injured him.'

'Gregory would have congratulated you too. Particularly when it comes to Frederick,' chuckled Lady Beatrice.

Alexandra joined in the laughter. 'So, Sir Marcus is not unique after all.'

'Unusual, yes, but not unique. I am pleased to hear that he likes your spirit.' Lady Beatrice was curious about Alexandra's reaction to Sir Marcus but decided not to pry. Instead, she enquired about the other potential matches. 'What about Mr Darcy and Lord Bassington? What did you speak about?'

'Books, travel, politics and philosophy.' Alexandra grinned when her aunt shook her head.

'Did you raise those subjects or did they?'

'Lord Bassington asked me what subject I would like to converse on while we danced. I returned the favour for Mr Darcy. Both of them seemed relieved when I gave them those options. I gathered that they are also not over-fond of the weather unless it affects the ability of their tenants to grow their produce.'

'Are any of them likely to call on you?'

'They might...'

'Will you encourage any of them?'

'I would like to get to know them better before I make that kind of a decision,' demurred Alexandra.

'Very well. You have plenty of time,' agreed her aunt.

The discussion made Alexandra consider one particular gentleman and his response after she told him that she was free to make her own choices. He seemed to become a little more reserved. Alexandra wondered why.

~~H~~

The next afternoon Lady Beatrice called on her friend Lady Cordelia, who had suggested the meeting at the ball.

After their greetings they settled comfortably in the informal parlour to enjoy their tea and chat.

Lady Cordelia enquired, 'did Alexandra enjoy the ball?'

'She did indeed. She was very complimentary on the quality of guests you invited,' replied Lady Beatrice with an indulgent smile.

'I admit I invited a number of the gentlemen to look them over because Theresa is coming out next season,' explained the hostess, whose daughter was rather nervous about having to deal with society.

'You are getting in early, my dear,' teased Lady Beatrice.

'As a matter of fact, it is rather late. Are you not aware that Theresa is nineteen? But because she was terrified of society, I gave her the extra time to gather her courage.'

'I had forgotten her age. Since she has not yet had her presentation, I kept thinking of her as younger. She is the same age as Alexandra.'

'That was why I wanted to check out the potential prospects – and the competition.' Now Lady Cordelia grinned at her friend. 'Did I notice your niece being rather taken with our neighbour, Beatrice?'

'I could not say. After all I do not know who all your neighbours are.' Lady Beatrice was intrigued.

'Sir Marcus owns the estate next to ours. Did you not know?'

'Considering I met the young man only the other night at your ball, no I did not.'

'He is keeping secrets again. Worthington and I had been friends with his parents until their tragic death. It must have been about three years ago. He sometimes played with Theresa when they were children, when he and his parents visited the Baron. The old Baron was Sir Marcus' uncle, who tragically, along with his heir, succumbed to the same illness as his parents during their last visit.'

The information about Theresa concerned Lady Beatrice. 'Do they still have a... connection?' she wanted to know.

'Rest easy, Beatrice,' laughed Lady Cordelia. 'Neither Theresa nor Marcus have any romantic interest in each other. I admit, I had hoped he would show an interest, but I do not believe they would suit. He needs someone much stronger than my daughter. Theresa needs a man who wants to cosset her, while Marcus needs a woman who will challenge him...' She left the question hanging.

'You mean someone like Alexandra.'

'Possibly. I had not thought of her before or I would have introduced them, but now that I have seen them together, I think they would suit very nicely. Has your niece said anything about him?'

'Not much. I know she enjoys his company, and she is intrigued by him. But she is cautious about sharing her feelings. Even with me,' replied Lady Beatrice. 'Apart from that, they have only met twice. It is much too early to speculate.'

'Maybe we should give them opportunities to get to know each other,' suggested Lady Cordelia. She smiled conspiratorially. 'I think I shall invite a few friends to an intimate dinner next week. Are you available next Tuesday?'

Lady Beatrice returned the smile. 'I believe we have no other engagements that evening.'

'Excellent. I look forward to your company.'

Having settled their immediate concerns, the two old friends continued their chat until Lady Beatrice had to take her leave.

~~H~~

On the agreed upon Tuesday, Lady Beatrice and Lady Alexandra were again guests at Worthington House.

They were warmly greeted by their hosts. Lady Cordelia said, 'I believe you know everyone here.'

They did know everyone, since it was indeed a small intimate dinner party with a few friends – a total of a dozen people. Even Lady Theresa Worthington was present.

Lady Cordelia had invited another couple of their contemporaries and a widowed uncle on her mother's side, who, although in his late fifties, was very debonair and enjoyed flirting with Lady Beatrice.

Their party was rounded out by one of Lord Worthington's newly married nieces, her husband and brother-in-law. And last, but not least, Sir Marcus was amongst the guests.

'Lady Alexandra, we meet again. Providence must be smiling upon me,' Sir Marcus greeted her.

'I believe providence had little to do with our invitation unless Lady Cordelia has changed her name. Shall we enquire?'

'There is no need, My Lady. I do not care by what name Providence likes to be known, as long as I again have the pleasure of your company.'

Alexandra laughed. 'You are in fine form tonight, Sir Marcus. Such flattery so early in the evening. You shall quite turn my head.'

'Nothing could be further from my mind. I speak nought but the truth.'

'In that case, Sir, let me assure you that my head is very firmly attached to my shoulders.'

They laughingly continued their banter until they were called to dinner.

Lord Worthington offered his arm to Alexandra to escort her to the table and seated her to his right.

That was the only true nod towards propriety and precedence. The others followed as they wished.

Alexandra was delighted to discover that her second dinner partner was Sir Marcus.

During dinner, she discussed politics with her host, while with Sir Marcus she argued the superiority of ancient Roman plumbing to modern English arrangements, or more accurately, the lack thereof.

Lord Worthington, who listened in on some of the conversation, shook his head and smiled. Those two were peas in a pod. They simply did not know it yet.

~~H~~

After dinner, the gentlemen had had their port and cigars, before they re-joined the ladies.

Sir Marcus immediately sought out Lady Alexandra to resume their conversation.

It was not long before they were in full flight again.

'And not only was their plumbing superior, but they also even managed to heat the floors of their villas,' argued Alexandra. 'Admittedly the climate in Italy is milder than in England but imagine not getting cold feet and being in a room that does not smell of smoke.'

'I must admit that sounds very exciting, although at times the smell of smoke is very welcome around some of my more odiferous acquaintances.'

'True, but that problem could be taken care of by improved plumbing,' Alexandra was not to be gainsaid.

'The servants would certainly appreciate not having to clear the fireplaces every day or carrying all those heavy cans of hot water, which is usually not so hot by the time it is in my bathtub,' Marcus was ready to officially concede her points. Privately he had agreed with her all along, but he enjoyed hearing her arguments.

'My father worked around that problem when he converted one of his dressing rooms into a bathing room. He had a copper installed and a pump to refill the copper and to add cold water to the bathtub. It may not be a perfect solution, but he was able to enjoy a hot bath whenever he felt like it,' explained Alexandra.

She did not mention that that bathing room was now her own. It would not do to lead the gentleman to think of herself undressed.

Her comment gave Marcus pause. A copper and a water pump in an upstairs room. Yes, he could see possibilities with that. He would think about this later, since now he was in the company of a charming lady.

Their conversation was interrupted by Lady Cordelia, who thought that they had monopolised each other enough for one evening. 'Lady Alex, would you be willing to entertain us on the pianoforte?' she asked.

'Gladly, Lady Cordelia. If you can tolerate my mediocre abilities.'

Alexandra selected a song that she had practiced enough to be competent and performed it quite creditably.

For the rest of the evening Alexandra enjoyed her conversation with the other guests, as Sir Marcus was now being diverted by Lord Worthington.

As they were leaving, Lady Beatrice extended an invitation to tea to Sir Marcus, who was pleased to accept.

~~H~~

One morning, Alexandra was awake very early, since she had not accepted any invitations for the evening before. She had felt that she needed a respite, since she suspected her aunt of meddling. It seemed that wherever she went, Sir Marcus was also in attendance. For a change, she wanted some time to herself.

Therefore, this morning she was eager to exercise Pegasus in Hyde Park. She dressed and had a hurried snack, intending to breakfast with her aunt on her return.

The morning was crisp and cool, despite the sun which had risen perhaps half an hour earlier. Alexandra breathed deeply in contented enjoyment as she made her way to Hyde Park, followed by the ever-present Larkin.

She was about to enter the gate at the start of Rotten Row when she encountered an acquaintance. 'Good morning, Mr Darcy.'

The young man coloured slightly at being addressed but raised his hat as he bowed in the saddle. 'Good morning, My Lady.' He looked as if he wanted to say something else but remained mute.

Darcy cursed himself. It was ever thus, that he did not know what to say to a lady, especially one whom he liked. The dances he had shared with her at the Worthington Ball, had been the best which he could remember. The conversation of Lady Alexandra had been delightfully lacking in overt flirting and fawning. She had spoken to him knowledgeably and as an equal, and he was considering calling on her. After all, as the daughter of an Earl, she was eminently suitable for him.

'Are you also here to exercise your horse? It is after all too early for the promenade.'

'Indeed, My Lady. Prometheus prefers the uncrowded road which this hour provides, and he is eager for a run.' As if to confirm this statement, Prometheus danced in place. 'I do not mean to be rude, but I hope that you will excuse me, while I let him work off his excess energy.'

'By all means, Mr Darcy. Enjoy your ride,' Alexandra responded pleasantly.

With a final nod, Darcy directed his horse onto Rotten Row, where Prometheus took off without prompting from his rider.

Pegasus let out a gentle nicker, indicating that he too wanted to run.

Since the trip from the house had warmed up his muscles, Alexandra gave him the signal to take off. Pegasus did not need a second invitation, as he went from a walk to a full gallop within a few strides.

Alexandra bent forward and raised herself slightly from the saddle to make the gallop easier for her mount. She laughed in exhilaration at the speed with which her stallion covered the ground.

About three quarters of a mile later, she overtook a startled looking gentleman.

Darcy could not decide what offended him the most. The fact that he was being overtaken by a woman, even though Prometheus was his fastest horse, or the unseemly display by that same woman, since her position made it very obvious that she had an exceedingly shapely posterior. He could not, of course, acknowledge even to himself that the sight was most appealing to his baser instincts.

As they approached the end of Rotten Row, Alexandra returned to an upright position, and gradually slowed Pegasus. She was still grinning and flushed with excitement when Darcy caught up with her.

'My Lady, pardon me for saying so, but do you think such a display is ladylike? Riding astride and in such a position...' He flushed as he remembered the sight of her... attributes, as she raced past him. 'Not all men are gentlemen, and might take your behaviour as an invitation to... ah...'

Alexandra laughed. 'Mr Darcy, please do not concern yourself. The advantage of riding astride is that I can outrace any gentleman, which I could not do if I was riding side-saddle; at least not without risking breaking my neck.'

Darcy was again affronted. He had meant well in pointing out that her behaviour was unacceptable to polite society. Instead of listening to and acting upon his advice, the lady laughed at him. Such an attitude was insupportable. 'Very well, My Lady, since you seem to be bereft of common decency, I shall no longer importune you with my presence.'

Darcy rode off in a huff, while Alexandra thought, that solves the problem of whether or not I want to get to know him better. I could never tolerate such a stuck-up prig.

~~H~~

12 *Friends old & new*

Sir Marcus was once again having tea with Lady Alexandra and Lady Beatrice.

It did not take long for him to be engrossed in conversation with Lady Alex. When the discussion led to their parents, they discovered that they had lost their parents in the same year. 'At least I was already an adult and had just finished my education, when illness claimed my parents' lives,' remarked Marcus.

He did not mention the additional blow that in that epidemic, he had also lost his uncle and cousin, who had been the previous Baron and his heir, respectively. At which point, he had to take on the responsibility for the Barony without warning. 'It must have been exceedingly difficult for you to be bereft of their guidance at such an early age.'

'It was, but I am grateful that guardianship of myself and my sister devolved, first to the Earl of Marven, and on his death to Lady Beatrice, rather than one of our less pleasant relatives.'

'You have a sister? Is she too young to be in town with you, since I have never met her?'

'Daphne is almost old enough to be presented, but she has no interest in anything so frivolous as balls and even conversations, if they are not concerned with science. She has very decidedly declared her preference for remaining at Herne Hyde with her tutor, making horrible messes in the laboratory which we had built for her.'

'You built a laboratory for her? She must be quite the bluestocking to have such particular interests. You and Lady Beatrice are most generous to indulge her so.'

'It has very little to do with indulgence, and rather more with self-preservation. Some of the smells they manage to create when they test various chemical reactions... Let us just say that they would make the house not fit to be lived in, for days at least.'

Marcus laughed. 'You sound just like my mother did when I developed an interest in science.'

'Did you also dabble in making interesting smells?'

'No. I prefer to deal with more conventional methods of creating heat. But I greatly admire Mr James Watt. And although my mother always feared that the boilers would explode, I think that his work with steam engines is sure to revolutionise industry.'

Alexandra was grateful that this was a subject upon which Daphne had waxed lyrical the previous year. While Alexandra a was not expert at it, she knew enough to contribute to the conversation. She found it fascinating that while Sir Marcus appeared to have several interests in common with her sister, he was not as completely absorbed by the subject. Instead, he seemed to have found a happy medium.

She was also pleased that Sir Marcus did her the courtesy of treating her as his intellectual equal, although she suspected that he had a slight advantage in that regard. But simply to be taken seriously by a man was unusual enough to be a huge point in his favour.

Alexandra found that the more time she spent in the gentleman's company, and the more they talked, the more she liked him. She felt that she could relax in his company, and he too seemed to let down his guard slightly, allowing her to see glimpses of the person behind the urbane façade.

As always, she was disappointed that the end of his visit arrived much too soon, and that the time they could spend together had flown past at a breakneck pace, as he was saying farewell again.

~~H~~

Alexandra was going for another morning ride, accompanied as always by Larkin, when she encountered an old friend.

'Good morning, My Lord.' Alexandra nodded and smiled impishly as she asked, 'who are you today?'

Lord Robert Flinter laughed and raised his hat in greeting. 'Good morning, Countess. At the moment I am myself, the poor second son, although while I am on leave in town, I will again appear to be my illustrious brother.'

'I gather that he is dodging fortune-hunters yet again?'

'Indeed, he is, and they are getting ever more determined. Since our father married at the age of twenty, and we have already reached our majority, they think that he must be ripe for the plucking.'

'Where is he in truth?'

'He is at Denton, looking after the estate.'

'If he is safe at Denton, why do you bother to pretend to be him?'

Robert had the grace to look somewhat shamefaced as he admitted, 'I am having fun disappointing all those rapacious ladies. Alistair is kinder than I am and would never consider being cruel.'

'Perhaps one of you is at last growing up, at least a little.'

'What can I say? It is enough for one of us to be sensible. Grandmother always claims that I have enough sense for adventure for both of us.'

'Your grandmother sounds like a woman of great sense.'

'She is indeed.' Robert sighed dramatically. 'Alas, her sensibility allows her to see much too clearly for my liking. Perhaps I should introduce you if the occasion arises. I believe you would get on exceedingly well.'

'I would love to meet your grandmother,' Alexandra replied honestly. The Duchess seemed to be very similar to her aunt. 'Were you trying to escape her scrutiny when you joined the army?'

'Not at all. I had planned to do so for years. You now have the honour of addressing Lieutenant Robert Flinter.'

'Congratulations, Lieutenant. But I must confess I was already aware of your new role, as one of the staunch defenders of our country.'

'Has Alistair pre-empted me by telling my news?'

'Not at all. Your secrets are safe with him. But I met one of your friends, Sir Marcus Scott.'

'You have met Marcus? How wonderful.' He paused as he tried to remember his last conversation with his friend. 'Were you the lady he mentioned in such glowing terms, who broke Marven's wrist?'

'I was that lady, but I must now reconsider my opinion about the gentleman since he exposed my secret.'

'He did no such thing. He never once mentioned your name. He simply described how much he admired the lady, who did not need rescuing. Although he seemed a little disappointed that he could not be your knight in shining armour. But hearing now that you two had met, and knowing your connection to Marven, I made the connection, if you pardon the pun.'

'Very well, I will consider forgiving him, but you were just as verbose that day. Contrary Countess, indeed.' Alexandra took on an expression of mock offense.

'Did I say that? I most humbly beg your pardon. Marcus had been plying me with some superb brandy, and I suppose my usual caution took a leave of absence. I believe Marcus mentioning this mystery woman's exploits, reminded me of another exceedingly independent lady.' He shrugged his shoulders and took on a mournful expression. 'What can I say. It was intended as a compliment.'

The lady relented and laughed at Robert's doleful countenance. 'Very well. Since I am feeling generous, I will forgive you too.'

Robert grinned. 'I appreciate your forbearance.' He changed the subject. 'What do you think of Marcus?'

Alexandra, caught off-guard, answered truthfully. 'I think he is wonderful company. I rarely have enjoyed someone's conversation as much as his.'

'I see. Is that how it is? As soon as I am out of sight, you forget all about me. I am devastated,' Robert exclaimed, clutching at his heart theatrically. 'While I am risking my life, defending our country, you immediately find another pretty face to distract you. Oh, woe is me.'

'I am afraid that you will have to console yourself with all those ladies who are chasing after your brother.'

'You are a most heartless creature,' protested Lord Robert, valiantly suppressing a grin.

'You only have yourself to blame, putting me wise to your heartbreaking activities amongst the ladies.'

'I am surprised that I have not heard any screams of anguish from your rejected suitors. I am certain there must be many.'

Alexandra gave a sardonic chuckle. 'You might be surprised how quickly gentlemen lose interest when they discover that my title and my fortune will remain mine. Grandfather was very thorough when he had the patent changed. My future husband will not even be entitled to the income from the estate; financially, all he can get out of marriage to me is an allowance... to be specified by me.'

Robert joined in her laughter. 'I believe I must stop at White's to hear first-hand the chagrin of all those fortune-hunters.'

'I wish you would, and afterwards you can join my aunt and me for dinner and tell us all about it.'

~~H~~

Lady Alexandra and Lord Robert were not the only people enjoying the crisp morning in Hyde Park.

Sir Marcus too had felt the need to get some exercise. He was thrilled when he recognised Lady Alex in the distance, even though he could not see her clearly, he would recognise her posture, and the way she held her head, anywhere.

He broke into a big smile and was about to speed up to join her on her ride, when he belatedly realised that she was already in company. And that company was none other than Lord Robert Flinter.

He watched with envy the ease with which the two conversed. The brilliant smile, and the occasional laughter, which floated on the air, caused him the acutest of pain.

Seeing these two together, it was obvious to him that they were made for each other. The ease, the camaraderie, not to say the evident love he perceived. It could only be as he had feared. Robert, as the second son of a Duke was the perfect consort for a Countess suo jure.

Marcus called himself every kind of fool, for forgetting her rank and letting himself hope that she would consider him as a potential match. But as a lowly Baron he should have known that she would look amongst her peers in society. And yet, it was so easy to forget her rank when they talked.

The more he came to know the intelligent and kind person that the lady was, the more he was drawn to her. Marcus was not blind to her faults. Lady Alex was opinionated, stubborn and used to giving orders… and having them obeyed. But she was also caring, considerate and, even though that was a secondary consideration, breathtakingly beautiful.

But he had been right when he first met her. She was out of his league.

The only sensible thing to do, to avoid breaking his heart, was to leave as soon as possible, and try to forget her.

For once in his life, Sir Marcus acted like a coward. He would not be able to lie about the reason for his departure, when confronted with the direct gaze of Lady Alex, and he could not bear to see the relief in her eyes, if he told her that he was quitting the field.

Instead, he sent a note to Lady Beatrice, excusing his sudden departure with a supposed emergency at his estate. The same day he was on his way back to Vintington Vale.

Lady Beatrice wondered at the gentleman's sudden departure but was pleased that Alexandra accepted the reason at face value.

~~H~~

Robert made good on his promise. At dinner two days later, he regaled the ladies with his investigation at his club.

'You should have heard them, clucking like chickens.' He mimicked Lord Barton to perfection as he complained, 'what was Herne thinking, letting that chit inherit his title…' He chuckled before he added in imitation of Gerald Stone, '…and even worse, his fortune.'

Lady Beatrice wiped tears of laughter from her cheeks as she chided, 'you are a scamp, but very talented. I could just see those gentlemen…'

'It was not all bad. Richard Fitzwilliam was there too, and he told them that at least Herne was saved from their depredations.'

'I always knew that Matlock and his family had more sense than most of the others.'

Lord Robert did not stay late that night since he had to report back for duty the following day. His captain, one Captain Richard Fitzwilliam, would have been most unforgiving if Robert were late.

~~H~~

Alexandra had an unexpected visitor a few days later.

The Dowager Duchess of Denton arrived towards the end of polite visiting hours, requesting a private word with the Countess.

After the introductions, and the obligatory refreshments and polite conversation, the Duchess commented, 'I have heard about you from my grandsons, particularly Robert, and I was curious to meet you.'

Alexandra smiled as she replied, 'He did suggest that he should introduce us, and I must admit that I too was curious to meet you, since Lord Robert spoke of you with such affection.'

'Indeed? That does not sound like him.'

'I admit it was couched as complaints, and since I was teasing him at the time, he claimed that we would get on well.'

'That I do believe. But I came here to find out how you feel about him.'

'I have only met him a few times. During those encounters I thought him excellent company. He is intelligent, personable and has a delightfully wicked sense of humour.'

'I asked how you feel about him.'

'I like him a great deal.'

'And?'

'There is no *and*, Your Grace. As I said. I think your grandsons are delightful gentlemen, whose company I thoroughly enjoy. I believe we can be good friends, after all, we made a pact to protect each other.'

'But you have no other interest in either of them?'

'No, Your Grace, I do not.'

'Pity. I think you and Robert would have suited each other.'

'I am sorry to disappoint you, Your Grace.'

'It is not your fault. I was hoping to keep him out of that blasted war on the continent, but if you are not interested in him, it cannot be helped.'

'Your Grace, I too would prefer it if all of our men could stay safely at home, but if they must fight, I prefer to have them under the command of an intelligent officer. Do you not agree?'

The Dowager Duchess sighed but responded with a small smile of her own. 'I suppose that I have to agree when you put it in those terms.' She tilted her head to one side and said with an impertinent smile, 'if you are not interested in the son of a Duke, who is intelligent, handsome, rich and likeable, you either have impossibly high standards, or perhaps someone has already captured your interest.'

Alexandra blushed at the blunt question. Before she could prevaricate, the Duchess said, 'never mind, I will not ask his name.'

As she prepared to leave, she offered, 'if you ever need help, feel free to come to me. I promised Robert that I would keep an eye on you.'

~~H~~

13 *Discoveries*

It seemed to be a year for emergencies. Two weeks after the sudden departure of Sir Marcus, Lady Alex did receive an express, requesting her return to Herne Hyde.

Lady Alex and Lady Beatrice each dashed off a few quick notes, while their belongings were packed up, to inform their friends of their need to leave town. An hour later they were on the road.

Thanks to Mr Brown's foresight, arranging for fresh horses along the way, they arrived at Herne Hyde late the following afternoon, even though the last part of the journey had to be made at walking pace, due to the heavy downpour.

As soon as the carriage stopped, Alexandra jumped out and dashed into the house.

Someone must have been watching out for the carriage since Mrs Martin rushed into the foyer just as Alexandra entered.

'What is happening?' she demanded of Mrs Martin.

'Because of the rain there has been a landslide, which is blocking the river at the border to Edgemere, where it goes through the cutting. This is causing flooding of the west fields. Mr Brown is there, overseeing the work to remove the blockage.' Mrs Martin gave a precise report, not bothering with social niceties.

Alexandra appreciated that her housekeeper did not waste time. 'Thank you. I need a horse and someone to accompany me to the site.'

'I thought you might. Perkins is waiting for you in the stable with two saddled horses, and a raincape.'

~~H~~

Perkins tightened the girths, while Alexandra put on the raincape and unbuttoned the split in her riding skirt. As soon as both finished, they took off, with Perkins leading the way.

Fortunately for Alexandra's frayed nerves, it did not take too long to arrive at the site of the landslide, where Mr Brown, and surprisingly her sister, were supervising the work to remove the blockage.

They had to carefully wade through water to come to the slight rise where Daphne had made her observation post.

After the briefest of greetings, Alexandra asked, 'what are those men doing on top of the landslide?'

'They are dragging a modified plough to create a channel through which the river can flow,' Daphne explained absentmindedly, as she carefully watched their progress.

Alexandra looked at all the water surrounding them. 'I can understand that you want to get the river back where it belongs, but would it not be easier if you waited for the rain to stop?'

'Not at all. The rain is actually helping. It is keeping the mud soft and even washes some of it away.'

'If those men are dragging a plough, why are you not using horses?'

'Because the ground is too soft and unstable.'

'Do you have an answer for everything?'

'Of course, I do, Alex. After all, this was my idea.' Daphne grinned as she briefly glanced at her sister.

'If you have everything under control, why did you send for me?'

Mr Brown spoke up. 'I am afraid that was my doing, My Lady. I sent for you immediately after the landslide occurred. I did not realise that Lady Daphne would be able to come up with a possible solution. It was her idea to use that dredge.'

Daphne grasped Alexandra's hand. 'I might have discovered a solution, but I am still glad that you have come.' She grinned mischievously. 'If only to see that some of my ideas have merit and are exceedingly practical.'

'You wanted to show off?'

'I would not have put it like that... but I suppose that is one way of looking at it.'

'If this works, I will be happy to claim that I have the most brilliant sister in the kingdom.'

They continued to watch until the light was just starting to fade, when the men on top of the mudslide suddenly dropped whatever they were holding and came rushing to the shore of the river.

'They must have reached the waterline, and the river is now finishing our work,' Daphne exclaimed excitedly.

Daphne seemed to be correct in her evaluation, as Alexandra noticed a swirling in the centre of the dark mass, as the water, which was backed up behind the mudslide, mixed with the mud in the channel the men had created, and was forcing its way through the gap. As a result, the initial small channel was widened as the mud was washed downriver.

As they watched the river starting to reclaim its course, Alexandra saw one of the men slip and fall into the swirling mess. 'Oh, no,' she exclaimed in horror, thinking that it was poor repayment to the man for his heroic efforts, to lose his life at the completion of the task.

She heard someone shout, 'PULL!'

Mr Brown pointed towards a group of men who were hauling on a rope, and two others cautiously approaching the edge of the slippery mess, where a man's head appeared.

In short order, the man who had slipped was dragged into the relatively clean water of the backed upriver, where after a quick rinse, he was helped to his feet.

Alexandra expelled a breath she had not realised she had been holding, as Daphne said in a cheerful manner, 'you did not think that I would not have them take precautions, did you? That was the other reason for having men pull the dredge. They are easier to haul than a horse.'

'You expected someone to slip and fall into the mud?'

'Considering the footing they were dealing with, there was an eighty percent chance that someone would slip. The percentage would increase to ninety or more, once the water started to flow. Naturally, I had everyone secured with a rope to ensure no one would be swept away.' Daphne explained the situation in a matter-of-fact tone.

'Naturally,' Alexandra sighed and shook her head in consternation. She would never completely understand the scientific mind, even if that mind belonged to her beloved sister.

~~H~~

Considering how much water had pooled above the gap, the water level was slow to drop, once the obstruction had been breached, especially as it was still raining heavily. But the water-was slowly receding.

Since the light was fading quickly, and no more could be done until the water drained, everyone returned to their homes. Since most of the men were servants at Herne Hyde, they were greeted with warm blankets and hot food on their arrival.

Alexandra and Daphne were glad to have hot baths to warm up, before joining Lady Beatrice and Amelia for dinner.

Daphne grinned at Alexandra when she entered the dining room. 'Well?' she challenged her sister.

'Well, what?'

'Am I the most brilliant sister in the Kingdom?'

'I will tell you in the morning, after we inspect the situation, but I suspect that you might be.'

Daphne's pout was marred by the twinkle in her eyes, as she said, 'you are pedantic as always.'

Lady Beatrice and Amelia watched the sisters teasing for a short while, before the lady asked. 'I would appreciate it if you were a little less cryptic. What has happened.'

Over dinner, Daphne explained. 'If it were not for our money hungry neighbour, we would not have had a problem. He had all the trees, on the slope which adjoins the river, harvested at once. With all the rain we had in recent weeks, the ground softened and since there was nothing left to hold the soil in place, it turned to mud and slid into the river. Since there were rocks in that mess, it blocked the cutting.'

This explanation was frequently interrupted as she hungrily tucked into the hot food.

As she started to go into technical detail, Alexandra and Lady Beatrice exchanged a glance, before begging her to stop. 'Daphne, I am certain this is fascinating to someone with a love for such things, but your explanation is lost on your sister and me.'

'I am concerned only with results. When we left, the water-level was dropping, so Daphne's most *brilliant* solution seems to be working.' Alexandra smiled at her sister as she emphasised her praise, earning her a quick grin.

Since they were all tired, although for different reasons, The ladies all opted for an early night in a warm bed.

~~H~~

The next morning, they discovered that the rain had actually helped in clearing the obstruction of the river. The additional water had caused many of the rocks to be swept downriver, clearing the gap.

While the fields were still waterlogged, they did not have to wade through standing water as they inspected the damage.

The flooding had caused damage to a couple of tenant houses and barns, as well as several fences.

Alexandra threw herself into the work to restore her estate.

Despite the distractions of work, her mind wandered at times to a certain gentleman, as she wondered at the kind of emergencies with which he was dealing.

~~H~~

Alexandra and her aunt had come to London for yet another season.

This time they were accompanied by Daphne and Amelia, who had both turned eighteen years of age. While neither of the girls was interested in spending a season in London, as neither was particularly interested in marriage, they had agreed to a compromise.

They would come to Town to be presented and remain for a week or two. After which they would be allowed to return to Herne Hyde, to continue their studies.

~~H~~

The Countess of Herne was proud to present her younger sister to Queen Charlotte.

As Daphne curtsied, the Queen asked graciously, 'shall you be one of our shining lights this season?'

'I certainly hope not, Your Majesty. I pray that my sister will allow me to return home on the morrow.'

'If you have no wish to spend the season in Town, why did you come here?'

Daphne shrugged. 'It is the done thing, I am told, but from what I have seen so far, I believe that I would prefer to stay in the country.'

'You have no interest in society? Whyever not?'

Daphne blushed, and, at last remembering her lessons in manners, stammered. 'I... ah... would rather not say.'

The Queen looking intrigued, demanded, 'I would like to know your reasons. Truthfully.' When Daphne still hesitated, she waved at her attendants to back away and give her some privacy.

Daphne gave her sister a desperate look. Alexandra nodded with a resigned air.

Directing her attention back at the Queen, Daphne said softly, 'I find most people shallow, boring, and lacking in understanding. I also have no interest in getting married.'

The Queen, with years of experience in hiding her emotions, managed to smile pleasantly, as she declared loudly, 'you appear to be a most perceptive young lady. I wish you well, Lady Daphne.' She smiled and nodded in dismissal.

Daphne curtsied again and backed out of the room.

~~H~~

That evening, the ladies relaxed with a private dinner.

Daphne, relieved that her ordeal was over, chided her sister. 'You could have told me that the Queen has a sense of humour. I was terrified that I might offend her.'

'None of us knew,' Lady Beatrice defended her niece. 'I believe that such a situation has never arisen.'

'But if even the Queen dislikes the kind of society we have, why does she not change it?'

'Because no one has enough power to change human nature. Certainly not overnight, and probably never.'

'Oh... yes... I forgot.'

~~H~~

14 Showdown

1805

Lady Alex was frantic. Daphne and Amelia had returned to Herne Hyde the previous week, while she remained in London with Lady Beatrice, who insisted that Alexandra should peruse the marriage mart yet again.

During the afternoon, her aunt had gone out shopping with her companion, Mrs Hodges, when they had been beset by footpads.

Mrs Hodges had valiantly tried to protect her employer and friend and received a nasty blow to the face for her efforts. By the time the footman, who had gone to get the carriage, could intervene, Lady Beatrice had been knocked unconscious, and the footpad had made off with her reticule and a diamond brooch torn from her dress.

Lady Beatrice had been conveyed to their home and a doctor was sent for. Doctor Fisher was examining the still unconscious lady while Alexandra fretted.

True, her aunt was no longer her guardian, but Alexandra loved her for the care and support she had received from the lady since her parents had died.

At last, the doctor finished his examination and addressed Lady Alexandra. 'I believe she has suffered a fracture to her skull. She was lucky that her bonnet protected her from the worst effects of the blow, but I must caution you not to get your hopes up for her recovery.'

'Is there a chance that my aunt will recover?' asked Alexandra.

'There is a chance, of course, but there is no guarantee. It will depend on how quickly she regains consciousness. The problem is to get nourishment into your aunt. She may be able to swallow small sips of broth, but if she remains insensible for too long...'

'I understand, Doctor Fisher. Thank you for being honest with me.' Alexandra braced herself before asking, 'is there anything we can do for her?'

'Keep her quiet and try to feed her broth whenever she is able to take it. Apart from that, all you can do is wait and hope for the best,' responded the doctor.

~~H~~

The following day, while Alexandra was sitting with her aunt, there was a commotion at the front door.

The butler, Mr Martin, the younger brother of the butler of Herne Hyde, came rushing into Lady Beatrice's chamber where Lady Alexandra sat, reading to her aunt. 'My Lady, the Earl of Marven has forced himself into the house and demands to see you.'

Alexandra was startled. 'He cannot be foolish enough to think that with Aunt Beatrice unconscious that he can gain any advantage,' she mused aloud.

'The Earl brought a clergyman and several rough looking footmen with him,' said the butler, trying to present a calm façade.

Alexandra's face took on a cold expression. 'Please send a messenger to Lord Matlock and ask him to attend me with all haste. We need to take care of this nuisance, once and for all.' She glanced around the room and rushed to her aunt's writing desk. It was the work of only a few moments to dash off a note to the gentleman. 'Here, take this, and have it delivered. Your messenger will have to explain that I think the Earl of Marven might try to force me into a marriage for his convenience.'

The butler took the note and hurried off to see to its delivery. Meanwhile, Alexandra asked Mrs Hodges to care for her aunt.

She then took a deep breath and bracing herself for a confrontation, Lady Alex went downstairs to see her cousin still standing in the foyer.

'Good afternoon, Cousin Frederick,' she politely greeted the Earl, while she remained standing on the bottom step to give her the height advantage. 'What brings you so unexpectedly to my house on this occasion.'

'Cousin Alexandra, it has come to my attention that your guardian has become incapacitated,' said the Earl of Marven in a gloating manner. 'Therefore, as the heir of your previous guardian it is my responsibility to take control of your wellbeing and to ensure that your estate is properly managed.'

'What makes you think that you can run my estate better than I can, Cousin?' purred Lady Alexandra. If he were not so annoying, the Earl of Marven's behaviour would have been amusing. Unfortunately, in her concern for her aunt, Alexandra was in no mood to be amused. 'Especially when you consider that my estate is profitable, while you are heavily in debt. Do you not agree that that would indicate that I am a better estate manager than you are?'

'You are an impertinent little chit. That is what you are. Cousin Beatrice has obviously not taught you proper manners. It seems I was wise to come to take you in hand. Once we are married, I will teach you how to behave towards your betters.'

'What makes you think that you could teach me anything, since I still retain all my skills?' Alexandra asked with a pointed glance at his wrist. 'Apart from that, I would never marry you, Cousin Frederick. Even if you were the last man on earth.'

'As your guardian, it is my right to choose your husband. Since I cannot in good conscience inflict your impertinence on anyone else, I have decided to be magnanimous and take you for my own wife.' He now indicated a man who had stayed in the background. 'This is Reverend Partland, he will perform the ceremony.'

The Reverend performed a minimal bow towards Lady Alexandra. 'Your cousin has procured a special licence, My Lady. I can perform the wedding within the hour.'

'Reverend Partland, you have been misinformed. I will not marry this... man. Therefore, your visit was for nought.'

'My Lady, I beg to disagree with you. Since you are still a minor, the Earl, as your guardian has the right to dictate whom you shall marry,' the Reverend retorted. To him it was obvious that the Earl had been correct about the wilfulness of the young woman. It was high time that a husband took her in hand. Her attitude towards the gentleman was truly disrespectful.

'How much did he promise to pay you, to perform a wedding with an unwilling bride?' Alexandra asked.

The Reverend spluttered, 'how dare you…'

Alexandra ignored his interruption. 'You are incorrect about several things. According to the law if I do not agree to the wedding, any ceremony you perform is invalid, not to say illegal. Therefore, it is irrelevant what words you say, without my consent they are just empty words.'

'And if I were stupid enough to consent to the wedding, neither Marven nor you would get a penny from the Herne estate. It is entailed to the heir, who has complete control of all properties and funds.' She grinned at the shocked expression on the clergyman's face.

Alexandra gave a disdainful huff. 'The final point is that the Earl of Marven is not my guardian, regardless of what he might have told you.'

'As your nearest male relative, I am your guardian,' shouted the Earl, frustrated that the young woman would not succumb to his bullying. He had thought that without her aunt to back her up, she would not have the presence of mind to counter his arguments.

'No, you are not,' Alexandra responded calmly. 'You are neither my nearest male relative nor are you my guardian. I have no need for a guardian…'

'You are not yet one and twenty, therefore you are a minor and subject to a guardian. Since I went to the trouble to remove Lady Beatrice, you are in my charge,' thundered Frederick in frustration.

'No, she is not,' came a deceptively quiet voice from behind Frederick, who whirled around to deal with whoever had the temerity to interfere with his plans.

The newcomer bowed respectfully to Alexandra. 'Good afternoon, Countess Herne. It is delightful to see you again, despite the pollution in your house,' Lord Matlock smiled at the lady. He had arrived a few minutes earlier with several highly trained footmen and listened with interest to the interchange.

'Good afternoon, Lord Matlock. The pleasure is all mine,' Alexandra smiled pleasantly at the gentleman. 'I hope you have been here long enough to hear the Earl of Marven's last statement?'

'I have indeed. And so have several other witnesses.' He indicated the footmen, who stepped aside and revealed three other gentlemen.

The Duke of Langford stepped forward. 'Marven, you are a disgrace to the peerage.'

'What are you speaking of? I have come to ensure that Cousin Alexandra was taken care of. As is the duty of a gentleman towards the weaker sex.' Marven tried to justify his behaviour.

'You just admitted to harming Lady Beatrice, the Countess of Marven, thinking that her removal would open the way for you to take on guardianship of your very distant cousin,' the Duke reminded the Earl of Marven, who turned white. 'I will have charges brought against you in the House of Lords. Such conduct is unconscionable, not to mention actionable.'

'It was also in vain since the Countess is in charge of her own life.' The Earl of Matlock chuckled gleefully. 'I am speaking of the Countess of Herne, of course.'

Before he could continue, Frederick burst out, 'this cannot be. She is a minor. She cannot be allowed to defy my wishes.'

'As a fully invested and confirmed member of the peerage, she has legally been an adult since the age of eighteen. She has not had, or needed, a guardian for over two years,' explained the delighted Lord Matlock to a chagrined Lord Marven.

Upon hearing this, the Reverend Partland spluttered, 'how are you going to pay your debts to my family now that that ripe plum has slipped through your fingers?'

'Are you saying that you would have married an unwilling bride to this scoundrel for monetary considerations?' asked the second of Lord Matlock's witnesses.

Reverend Partland had not paid attention to the other witnesses until this one spoke. Now it was his turn to blanch. 'Your Grace,' he addressed Archbishop Langton, 'pardon me, I did not notice your arrival.'

'Obviously, or you would have guarded your tongue. You will wait on me tomorrow, when we will discuss your future,' the disgusted Archbishop advised the Reverend.

'Your Graces,' the final member of their party spoke up. 'We can save a lot of trouble if you would allow me to meet these... ah, gentlemen on the field of honour tomorrow morning.' Sir Marcus had been visiting with Richard Fitzwilliam and insisted on coming along when he found out who had sent the urgent message.

'No,' gasped Alexandra.

'Absolutely not,' insisted the Archbishop and the Duke.

'I would not want you to besmirch your hands dealing with this scum,' agreed Lord Matlock.

Sir Marcus looked disappointed. 'Pity, but if you insist...' He looked at the other men, as if hoping they would change their minds.

'We insist,' they all agreed.

'Now that that is settled,' declared Lady Alex. 'May I offer you some refreshments, My Lords.' Alexandra was smiling pleasantly at the four gentlemen who had come to her assistance. When they agreed, she turned to her butler who had quietly stood behind her the entire time and requested with a smirk. 'Please bring refreshments to the library, after you throw out the garbage. I feel certain that Lord Matlock's staff will assist you, if necessary.'

~~H~~

Alexandra led the way to the indicated room with her four welcome guests. Once they were in private, she thanked them. 'Gentlemen, I am grateful for your assistance. While it is true that my cousin could not have forced me to marry him, things could have turned rather unpleasant. I am in your debt.'

'Think nothing of it, my dear,' declared the old Duke with a smile. 'It is the most fun I have had in ages. I always knew Marven was an idiot, but I did not think he would go this far. Injuring a lady for his own gain. It is beyond the pale.'

'*Can* something be done in the House of Lords?' enquired Alexandra.

'He admitted injuring your aunt, who is also a member of the peerage, either himself or by proxy. I am hoping we can have him hanged. Apart from Gregory and his wife, the whole family is rotten. It would be best to remove them from any position of influence.'

The Archbishop reluctantly agreed, 'harsh but true.'

Alexandra looked questioningly at the cleric and then at Lord Matlock, who realised that the lady was not acquainted with his whole party. He performed the introductions and then explained to Alexandra, 'I gave them the outline of your background on the way over.'

'Thank you, Lord Matlock. But to get back to my cousin. If I understand the law correctly, if he is found guilty, his title can be revoked, not just from him, but the whole family.'

'That would be a boon for society at large. That family is rotten to the core,' declared the Duke.

'Do not worry, my dear,' said the Earl of Matlock. 'We will take care of that viper. How is your aunt?'

'Thank you, My Lord. Doctor Fisher says there is a chance she will recover, but he has no guarantees,' replied Alexandra with a sigh.

Mr Martin entered the library with the tea trolley. After serving her guests, Alexandra discussed with them the steps they planned to take.

Soon the older gentlemen took their leave to make good on their promises.

~~H~~

15 Recovery

Sir Marcus stayed behind for a private word with Alexandra.

'Are you truly well?' he asked, concerned.

'I am not as unaffected as I led my cousin to believe,' admitted Alexandra. 'But I will be in better spirits when my aunt recovers, and that man has paid the price for injuring such a dear lady.'

'I do not think you need to worry. I have never seen those gentlemen as angry before. All of them are great believers that it is their duty to protect ladies.'

'Yes, they were quite my knights in shining armour.' Alexandra smirked. 'But I was happy to hear they had more sense than you. What were you thinking? Offering to duel Marven. You could have been hurt or even killed.'

'I do not think so. Marven is a coward and a bully; and more interested in debauchery than practice.' Marcus decided that a change of topic was called for. 'On the way over, I discovered that you are quite mendacious. You led everyone to believe that Lady Beatrice was your guardian,' teased Sir Marcus.

'She was my guardian. But we agreed that it would be more politic to let society think that I still needed her guardianship. It slowed down some fortune-hunters since they expected my aunt to be more astute than a young lady. But now I am worried that this pretence may cost my aunt her life.' Alexandra was still distraught.

'Have faith, dear lady. Your aunt has a strong constitution and a zest for life. I am convinced that she will recover. If only to hear the screams of anguish when society finds out that you two have pulled the wool over their eyes for years.'

At last, his joking had the desired effect. Alexandra smiled at him. 'Thank you for cheering me up. But if you would excuse me, I am anxious to get back to that lady, to do what I can to make your words come true.'

~~H~~

As Marcus strolled back to Matlock House, his mind returned from the last few hours to the last twelve months.

Over the past year, since he left London so precipitously, he had thrown himself into his work, to try to keep his mind from the enchanting young woman, who had captured his imagination and his heart.

But neither work nor study had helped. Lady Alexandra intruded not only on his waking hours, but also his dreams. He wondered how long it would take for Robert to court and marry her. He was torn whether to hope it would be soon, to remove her from being a temptation, or later, as in never, so that he would not have to think of her married to someone else.

Marcus could hardly believe how quickly he had become enamoured with the lady. They had not met above two dozen times, but he had to admit to himself that he had fallen hopelessly in love with Alexandra.

And it was hopeless. She might see him as a friend, but she could not possibly consider him as a serious contender for her hand. And even if she could be convinced, which he greatly doubted, since he had nothing to offer her which she did not already possess and more, but Lady Beatrice would surely not allow her ward to tie herself to him.

The first time, after his departure from London, when he received a letter from Robert, Marcus had procrastinated opening the missive for several days, afraid that his friend would announce his engagement. Eventually he had to know, and he broke the seal. Robert did indeed write about engagements, but they were of a martial kind, rather than marital.

Without betraying any details, Robert informed him that he had been sent to fight, and there was not the slightest hint of a personal involvement in the letter.

The situation had continued for a year. Two weeks ago, Marcus could not put it off any longer. He had to come to London for estate business, and today he had paid a visit to Richard Fitzwilliam, a mutual friend of his and Robert's, who was on a short leave.

Marcus had been on his way out of Matlock House when Lady Alexandra's footman had just delivered his message to the Earl. Since Marcus overheard where the Earl and his companions were bound, he could not help himself, he had followed along.

He had been shocked to learn that Lady Beatrice was no longer Lady Alexandra's guardian. In truth, she had not been in that role for the two years he had known the ladies. Marcus could intellectually understand the explanation Alexandra had provided but was chagrined that she had not trusted him enough to tell him the truth.

Did she consider him a fortune-hunter?

The thought was unpalatable.

He had to remind himself that she did not know him well enough to make that kind of judgement.

Perhaps, while they were both in town, he would have the opportunity to strengthen their friendship at least.

~~H~~

Alexandra returned to her aunt's side and used the quiet time to ponder the happenings of the previous hour.

She was amazed at the strong reaction she had had when Sir Marcus offered to duel her cousin. She had been terrified that the gentleman might be hurt, or worse, killed.

She tried to imagine several other gentlemen of her acquaintance in that position. While she was mildly concerned about their wellbeing, as she would be about anyone who might be in harm's way, the thought did not cause the anxiety she had experienced with Sir Marcus.

The gentleman greatly confused her. He appeared to enjoy her company. At times during their conversations, he relaxed his reserve and became animated, even allowing her glimpses behind his polite public persona. When that happened, she felt a spark, a connection which made her catch her breath.

At other times, his reserve was fully in place, and although his conversation was interesting and pleasant, he was shuttered and withdrawn.

Sometimes he seemed interested in her, at other times he was formally polite. It seemed almost like he enjoyed her company as a friend but was trying not to raise her expectations.

It was most frustrating, particularly since she found herself thinking about him frequently in terms other than friendship. She was in serious danger of losing her heart to him but was afraid that it was a hopeless dream.

Looking at her aunt lying in her bed so very still, she decided that she had enough concerns at present, and would not let herself be distracted with things she could not control.

~~H~~

The following morning Lady Beatrice regained her senses, and a week later the doctor allowed her to leave her bed and join her niece in the drawing room on the condition that she did not exert herself.

'Doctor Fisher has very decided opinions,' complained Lady Beatrice. 'He only allowed me to come downstairs, if I promised to sit quietly and not exert myself.'

'Aunt, a week ago I did not know whether you would live or die. I should hope you would be sensible enough to take it easy and take care of your health. For my sake if not for your own,' scolded Alexandra.

'I must be getting better since you feel free to scold me,' grinned her aunt. 'Now tell me all the news you have been withholding during my convalescence.'

'Not much has happened unless you count that I rejected a marriage last week,' teased Alexandra.

'Who proposed to you,' asked a surprised Lady Beatrice.

'No one proposed as such. The day after your attack, Cousin Frederick simply insisted that I should marry him within the hour... irrespective of my wishes. He had made this clergyman believe that with you incapacitated, he had the right to make decisions for me.' Alexandra laughed.

'I gather you managed to convince him otherwise.'

'I did indeed, although I had some assistance.' Alexandra now related the whole incident to her aunt.

Lady Beatrice was angry when she heard that her cousin had arranged the attack but was satisfied that Frederick would face the consequences of his actions.

'I am relieved that you did not try to deal with the situation on your own,' praised Lady Beatrice.

'I may be proud of my independence, but I am not stupid, or even reckless. When I have to deal with a misogynist like Frederick, I know he will not listen to anything I have to say. Luckily, Lord Matlock's house is almost next door, and I knew him to be in residence. I am grateful that he was at home and willing to come immediately.'

'Yes, he has always been a good friend. Now, what else has been happening?'

The ladies spent a pleasant afternoon chatting, as Lady Beatrice caught up on recent events.

~~H~~

Two days later, Doctor Fisher informed the ladies, that while Lady Beatrice was out of danger, the injury had taken its toll, and it would be advisable if the lady were to remove to the country, to complete her recovery.

Lady Beatrice was reluctant to leave town since the purpose of the visit was to allow Alexandra to meet with potential suitors. Her niece on the other hand, was delighted with the idea, especially as they had had an awkward visit the previous day.

Sir Marcus had come to call, ostensibly to enquire about Lady Beatrice's condition. Although on the surface the conversation had been pleasant, Sir Marcus had used words like friend and friendship much too often for Alexandra's liking.

It was becoming clear to her that although the gentleman liked her, he was obviously trying to manage her expectations. The realisation hurt, and she wanted time away from the pressure of the season's marriage mart to consider her options.

In the end, the doctor and Alexandra prevailed, and the ladies quit Town, travelling to Herne Hyde in easy stages.

Lady Beatrice managed to get one concession from her niece. Since Alexandra was missing out on the opportunity to interact with eligible gentlemen, she would issue invitations for a house-party, to be held over the summer months at Herne Hyde.

~~H~~

They had been back at Herne Hyde for a fortnight when Lady Beatrice confronted her niece.

'Alexandra, what is going on with you. You have been alternately moping, or losing your temper, snapping at people. To be honest, I worry more about the latter than the former.'

'I have not…' Alexandra snapped to deny the accusation.

'You have indeed.' Lady Beatrice gave her a pointed look.

As Alexandra was preparing herself for another sharp riposte, she caught herself, realising what she was doing. At that point, the fight went out of her. 'I am sorry, Aunt.' She sighed, as she calmed a little more. 'I have been quite distracted lately.'

'So I noticed. What, or should I say who, is the reason for your unreasonable behaviour. It is quite unlike you.'

Alexandra hesitated, before admitting, 'a gentleman of my acquaintance, of whom I have become rather fond, does not reciprocate my feelings.'

'I must disagree with you, Alexandra. Sir Marcus does seem quite smitten with you.'

'Aunt, please stop. He has made it quite clear that he is only interested in me as a friend.'

'I believe that friendship is a wonderful basis for marriage.'

'Aunt, while I agree with you in principle, how often do I have to repeat that for some people, friendship alone is not enough.'

'Perhaps you and he just need more time to work things out.'

~~H~~

A few days before the guests for their house-party were to arrive, Lady Beatrice received a letter from Lord Matlock.

The missive informed her that the Earl of Marven had been tried for the attempted murder of Lady Beatrice in the House of Lords.

Due to the impeccable witnesses who had heard his confession at Hunt House, the verdict had been almost unanimous, with only a few abstentions. He was sentenced to be hung, a sentence which had been carried out the day before.

As a consequence, the family, except for Lady Beatrice had been stripped of all titles, and the Marven estate, at least what was left of it, had been confiscated by the crown.

He added almost as an aside that Reverend Partland had been defrocked and stripped of his living.

Lady Beatrice, who read the letter to her niece, chuckled as she read the last paragraph. 'We will be keeping an eye on those Lords who did not find Marven guilty. This is too good an opportunity for some house-cleaning.'

~~H~~

16 House-party

The guests started to arrive at Herne Hyde, where Lady Alexandra and Lady Beatrice were ready to receive them. They had invited a number of friends, including Lady Alex's favoured companions, to visit for a few weeks.

The first to arrive were Lord and Lady Worthington, accompanied by their daughter Theresa.

The hostesses greeted their guests most warmly. 'We are hoping to keep this party quite informal, to give the young people a chance to actually get to know each other,' explained Lady Beatrice.

The two matrons had been on a first name basis for decades, when in private. They now extended that privilege to the two young women.

Lord Worthington was feeling expansive when he addressed Alexandra. He offered with a smile, 'since we are going to be informal, just call me Worthington.'

'Thank you, Worthington. You are being too kind.' Alexandra smiled at the gentleman with twinkling eyes. 'In that case, please call me Herne.'

Worthington did a double take. Ladies were not addressed by the name of their title; it was simply not the done thing. But he decided to go along with the lady's joke. 'Thank you, Herne, I shall be delighted to do so, and I am exceedingly pleased that we understand each other.'

He was rewarded by a delighted smile from the young lady and a chuckle from his wife, who claimed, 'I think I shall have to keep score. So far, it seems to be a draw.'

The others joined in her laughter. 'I think we shall have a most amusing time during your visit,' opined Lady Beatrice.

~~H~~

Over the next few days more visitors arrived. There were a few couples of Lady Beatrice's generation, or slightly younger, who accompanied their daughters, or in the case of Mrs Mornington, a childhood friend of Lady Beatrice, who brought her two nieces.

Since gentlemen did not need the chaperonage of their parents, Lady Beatrice had decided to extend the invitation to them directly. All of them were in their twenties or early thirties. Most of them were younger sons and had a good reputation in society.

This house-party was designed to give the young people more opportunity to converse, without the pressure of all the society gossips watching them at all times.

Although Lady Beatrice did not push her niece to find a husband, she was getting a little concerned that after three seasons, Alexandra had still not made a suitable match with whom to continue the Herne lineage.

Alexandra had shown a distinct preference for Sir Marcus, and Lady Beatrice was convinced that he had feelings for Alexandra, but he appeared to have some reason for holding back. In an effort to find out the reason, she invited the gentleman. Perhaps if he saw Alexandra being courted by other men, he would overcome his hesitation.

Lady Beatrice hoped that, even if Alexandra and Marcus could not come to an understanding, Alexandra would at least settle on one of the other prospects. To that end she had invited a number of gentlemen of whom Alexandra had spoken well, after meeting them in London. She had considered extending an invitation to Mr Darcy, but Alexandra vetoed the idea. 'I do not believe that he would be comfortable in such informal company,' she declared.

Lady Beatrice had managed to convince Daphne and Amelia to put aside their studies for the duration of the visit. The addition of the two young women, had allowed the lady to invite two further gentlemen, to even out the numbers. Lady Beatrice did not expect either Daphne or Amelia to be interested in any of them, but it increased the number of choices for Alexandra.

~~H~~

Alexandra thoroughly enjoyed most of the first dinner, when the party was fully assembled. She sat at the head of the table, with Lord Worthington on her right and Lord Bassington on her left.

'Have you been following the discussion in the House of Lords regarding Atholl's claim for compensation from the Isle of Man, Herne?' Lord Worthington asked his hostess.

Alexandra was entertained that both the subject and Worthington's style of address caught Lord Bassington by surprise, judging by the looks he was giving them.

'I have indeed. Personally, I would have thought that claiming compensation forty years after his father sold his sovereignty over the island to the crown, is rather rich, especially since the former Duke thought that he had been adequately compensated. But I suspect the current Duke has better friends than his father.'

They fell into a discussion of the finer details of the bill which had just been passed, with Bassington trying to listen to the conversation, while engaging his other dinner partner in a discussion of the latest gossip from London.

During the second course, Lord Bassington was at last able to converse with Alexandra. 'Lady Alexandra, I was aware that you had an interest in current affairs, but I did not realise you were quite so knowledgeable about politics.'

'I suppose it could have been misconstrued that when I spoke of current affairs, I meant that I was well informed about who had a new mistress. While one cannot avoid hearing about such affairs, I find politics much more absorbing. After all, politics can affect my interests.'

'I imagine your interests are also affected by the problems we are having with France. I expect that you too are hoping that our navy can keep Mr Bonaparte away from our shores.'

After some minutes of discussion, Alexandra commented, 'you appear to be remarkably well informed, Lord Bassington.'

'Since my older brother is in the Royal Navy, and various cousins serve in the army, it is a subject that greatly interests my family.'

This statement led to a conversation about their respective families.

~~H~~

Another member of Alexandra's family had an enjoyable evening. Daphne discovered to her delight that her dinner partner was Sir Marcus.

She lost no time informing the gentleman, 'my sister tells me that you are an admirer of Mr James Watt, and his steam engines.'

'I am indeed. I believe that his steam engines will revolutionise manufacturing in our country.' Marcus replied, grateful that his dinner partner could distract his mind from the lady at the head of the table.

He had accepted the invitation to the house-party with mixed feelings. Part of him was uncertain whether he could stand watching Alexandra being courted by any of the other men, but the rest of him wanted the pleasure of Alexandra's company.

'Not just manufacturing, mining as well.' Daphne became excited to have someone with whom she could discuss one of her pet subjects. 'Did you know that last year Mr Trevithick's steam locomotive hauled a train along the tramway of the Penydarren Ironworks in Wales?'

She and Sir Marcus became so engrossed in their discussion, they forgot about the other guests, as they exchanged ideas how some of the latest inventions could be applied to everyday life.

It turned out that Sir Marcus had a wonderful evening. His conversation with Lady Daphne had been intellectually stimulating.

Due to the fact that he had no interest in the young lady, beyond their common interests, he was able to relax and simply enjoy the conversation. He would have been shocked to realise how his interest was being perceived.

~~H~~

Even though Daphne and Marcus paid little attention to the other members of their party, several people noticed the animated conversation between the two.

Lady Alexandra felt a stab of disappointment and even jealousy, when she noticed the enjoyment which her beloved sister derived from the company of Sir Marcus. Judging that their similar interests made them more compatible, she at last understood why Sir Marcus had never seen her as more than a friend.

For the rest of the evening, she was most determined to ignore her breaking heart, although when she was alone in the sanctuary of her bedroom, she cried herself to sleep.

~~H~~

The morning was clear and bright, but still pleasantly cool for the time of year. After a restless night's sleep, Alexandra took Pegasus out for a ride.

She had decided that since most of the guests kept town hours, she could attend to her duties in the early morning hours. This morning she planned to check out the west fields to see for herself how they fared after the previous year's flood. The reports had been excellent, but she wanted to see for herself.

Alexandra was racing along a path, letting Pegasus enjoy a good run, when she spotted another rider ahead of them. Her face lit up as she recognised Sir Marcus, until she remembered the interest Daphne and the gentleman had displayed in each other the previous evening.

By the time Marcus turned, at hearing Pegasus' hoofbeats, Alexandra had her emotions and features under control, and displayed a politely pleasant smile.

When Marcus recognised the rider, he unconsciously broke into a wide smile, until he saw the expression on Alexandra's face. He could not help the momentary disappointed look, which flashed across his countenance, at seeing the polite smile.

Alexandra in turn saw the disappointment and attributed it to Marcus hoping to see her sister, rather than herself.

Instead of slowing down to chat with Marcus, as she dearly wished to do, she simply nodded as she raced past him.

She attributed the tears, which started to trickle down her cheeks, to the wind, caused by the speed of her ride, irritating her eyes.

~~H~~

Marcus, who had thought to escape the house into the crisp morning air, in the hope to clear his thoughts, was shaken by the chance meeting. Alexandra had only given him a polite smile and a nod as she raced past him.

It was obvious from that encounter that she saw him merely as a pleasant acquaintance. It seemed hopeless that she would ever return his feelings.

He pondered his options.

What if he spoke to Alexandra and declared his love for her? Would she respond favourably and consider him as a suitor, or...

Since he was wool-gathering, his horse had started to amble back towards the stable. As he was passing an isolated building, some distance from the main house, he was hailed by a female voice.

Marcus was startled out of his reverie, as he recognised the young lady. 'Lady Daphne, I had not expected to find you here.'

'You will not give me away, will you?'

'No, of course not. But what are you doing here?'

'I am hiding from a gentleman, who seems to think that I am looking for a husband and would not believe me when I told him I had no such inclination.' She sighed and rolled her eyes. 'Especially with him. He has only been here for two days, but in those days, he has managed to make quite a pest of himself.'

'Please forgive me for asking, but do you not have a wish to marry?' Since it looked like they would have an extended conversation, Marcus dismounted.

'Since you asked a most improper question, may I be equally improper?'

Marcus chuckled. 'By all means, feel free to be as improper as you like.'

'Why would I wish to put myself in the power of some mentally challenged man? I am not certain that particular pest knows how to count above ten without taking off his shoes. My sister has generously offered to support me in whatever I wish to do. Since I shall never need to marry for financial security, I can remain single and pursue my own interests. And enjoy my life.'

'That is a most unusual attitude. I was under the impression that all young ladies wish to marry.'

'I am certain that many do wish to marry because most women would like to have children. But many only marry because it is the only way for them to have a roof over their head and food on the table.'

'Surely it cannot be that bad?'

'How would you like to become property on the occasion of your marriage, with no rights of your own? Having to obey your spouse's wishes and even whims, no matter how ridiculous or unpleasant.'

'I would hate it,' Marcus conceded. 'Is it truly that bad? I must admit that I had never considered the rules under which women in our country live.'

'So, you can understand why I would not want to give up my freedom to make my own choices. It would be intolerable to be shackled to some man, who thinks that simply by being a man, he is more intelligent than I am, when nothing could be further from the truth.'

'You have a very high opinion of your intelligence.'

'It is but the truth.' Daphne shrugged dismissively, before she broke into a wide grin. 'Thanks to Alexandra, I do not have to pretend to be something I am not.'

Marcus laughed in response to the unrepentant attitude of the young woman. 'You are fortunate indeed, to have such an understanding sister. She is a most exceptional woman.'

'Yes, I know. I must admit that I feel sorry for her. In her position she must marry and produce an heir. I just wish she would find someone she truly likes, and who would treat her with the respect she deserves.'

'Perhaps she has already met someone, but the time is not right.' Marcus remembered seeing Alexandra with Lord Robert, and the ease of their interactions.

Daphne sighed as she shook her head. 'I just wish I knew what she is looking for. I am certain that I would be able to help her find the right man.'

Marcus chuckled sadly. 'I do not believe the scientific method can deal with such elusive things like love, since it cannot be measured or quantified.'

'I never understood love. At least not the kind of love that would make somebody want to marry.'

'I believe that nobody can explain the unexplainable. But since we cannot fathom the unfathomable, may I escort you wherever it is you are going?'

'I suppose with you escorting me, it will be safe enough for me to return to the house.'

'It will be my pleasure.' Marcus offered Daphne his arm, while holding onto the reins with his other hand. 'Since we cannot solve the conundrum of love, perhaps we can solve more solid problems?'

As they strolled back to the house, they resumed their companionable conversation from the previous evening.

~~H~~

17 Conversations

Marcus and Daphne arrived just in time to meet their neighbour, Mr Harper, who had offered to take the gentlemen shooting, which most of the gentlemen accepted with pleasure.

One of the gentlemen, who had chosen to remain behind, was the Right Honourable Mr Cedric Clifford. He had been one of the first guests to arrive and had almost immediately singled out Lady Daphne as his perfect companion in life. She was young, beautiful, and most importantly, was sure to have an excellent dowry.

Admittedly, Lady Herne had all these qualities and more, but the rumour was that when she married, she would remain in control of her fortune. Initially he had thought that the right man, one such as himself, could charm the lady into being a compliant wife, who could be persuaded to hand over control to her husband; an hour in her company had disabused him of that notion. Therefore, Lady Daphne was a better choice.

He had been most put out, when on the previous evening, the lady had completely ignored him in favour of Sir Marcus. Now that the other gentlemen had gone to enjoy their sport, he saw his opportunity to hunt fairer game.

He found his prey on the terrace, in the company of Lady Theresa and the Mornington sisters. The ladies rose as they exchanged greetings. He bowed to Daphne and requested, 'Lady Daphne, would you care to stroll about the gardens?'

'I thank you for the offer, Mr Clifford, but I prefer to stay here.'

'Come, Lady Daphne, it is a beautiful day, which is simply made to be enjoyed by a stroll about the gardens.'

'I can enjoy it just as well from the terrace, Mr Clifford.'

'But I was hoping that you could tell me about the delightful flowers you have in the garden. There are some which I have never seen before.'

'If you are interested in botany, I would be pleased to send for the gardener to tell you all about them.'

'Ah, but the explanations would be much more memorable if they came from your lips.'

'But therein lies the rub, Mr Clifford. I have no interest in flowers and would be unable to satisfy your thirst for knowledge.'

'My apologies, Lady Daphne, I should have realised that a gentle lady like yourself would not wish to clutter her mind with such esoterica. I shall be content to simply enjoy the beauty of those blooms, even though your own beauty outshines them all.'

'Mr Clifford, are you saying that you believe me to be incapable of learning, what you call, esoteric subjects?'

'My dear Lady Daphne, there is no shame in not being an intellectual giant. It is a well-known fact that ladies are simply not made to understand the intricacies of natural philosophy.'

'Mr Clifford, tu es intellectualis pumilio. Quoniam in novissimo tempore non sum interest in est cum ducitur per viam horti vel huc atque illuc, a te. (*Mr Clifford, you are the intellectual midget. For the last time. I have no interest in being led up the garden path, or anywhere else, by you.*'

'I beg your pardon, what did you say?' Clifford spluttered. The last thing he had expected was to be insulted and told off in Latin.

'I thought that all gentlemen were supposed to have at least a basic understanding of Latin. You are obviously incapable of grasping even basic concepts, such as, when a lady is not interested in your company.' Daphne dipped a minimal curtsy. 'Now if you will excuse me, I have better things to do than argue with you.'

Clifford reached out to grab Daphne's arm, when a cold voice stopped him. 'I recommend that you do not lay a hand on my sister, otherwise you will be incapable of ever using it again.'

He whirled around to be confronted by Lady Alexandra, flanked by two large footmen. As Clifford gaped at her, Alexandra added with a sardonic smile, 'it is such a shame that you have to cut short your visit, Mr Clifford. You may be sure that I will pass on your apologies to my other guests.'

After their guest was escorted to his room to pack by the footmen, Daphne hugged her sister. 'Thank you. But how did you know that I needed help?'

'When Clifford would not take no for an answer, Theresa raised the alarm,' Alexandra explained.

'The nerve of that man, to think I could be interested in him.' Daphne was still angry as she huffed, 'ladies are simply not made to understand the intricacies of natural philosophy.'

She took a deep breath to calm herself. 'I think I had better go and thank Theresa.'

~~H~~

The atmosphere improved significantly for the Hunt sisters, after the departure of Mr Clifford.

'Aunt Beatrice, why did you want to invite Mr Clifford? Did you not know how persistent that man could be?' Alexandra enquired when she had a chance, during the separation of the sexes, after dinner.

'I am sorry, my dear. That aspect of his character must be a new development. He always had a reputation for being urbane.'

'I might be able to shed some light on the subject,' offered Mrs Mornington. 'I heard a rumour that his family has made a bad investment and lost a significant amount of money. Mind you, that is only a rumour.'

'If he is desperate for funds, that would explain his new persistence, I suppose.' Lady Beatrice eyed her old friend with amusement. 'You always had exceptional sources. Do you know if any of our other guests might be as persistent?'

'No more than is usual for second sons since most of them are rarely well provided for by their parents.' Mrs Mornington gave her hostesses an impish smile. 'I must say though, your family seems to have snared the most eligible bachelor amongst your guests. Not only is he the only son, but he reputedly has quite a significant fortune.'

'So, we are assured that at least one of the gentlemen is not a fortune-hunter,' Alexandra laughed at the lady's comment.

'Please, my dear, no gentleman of the first circles is a fortune-hunter. They are simply conserving the wealth in their families.'

'Of course. How cynical of me to think anything else.'

'I am glad that you understand.'

~~H~~

On her way to bed, Alexandra was passing her aunt's sitting room when she heard the murmur of voices followed by laughter. She was pleased that her aunt had invited her oldest friend to be a part of the house-party. It seemed that Mrs Lucinda Mornington was just the tonic Lady Beatrice needed for a full recovery from her attack.

Alexandra might have been amazed, or possibly amused by the topic of conversation between the ladies.

Lady Beatrice and Mrs Mornington were reminiscing about their childhood.

'Lucy, do you remember that summer when we found that slow worm and put it in your governess' bed?'

Mrs Mornington laughed at the reminder. 'I do indeed, Trixie. She was most put out. She claimed that we were devil's spawn, planning to kill her with a death adder.'

'For a woman who was supposedly so very educated, she could not even tell the difference between a lizard and a snake.' Lady Beatrice chuckled. 'Although she did give us the opportunity to discover new shades of red, as she went from pale all the way to a lovely shade of puce.'

'At least mother was prepared to accept that I needed a governess who could teach more than just how to walk elegantly and pour tea. Miss Finch, who replaced her, was a great improvement.'

The ladies continued their walk down memory lane until the early hours. Lady Beatrice might have missed out on sleep but was compensated by a feeling of contentment.

~~H~~

Alexandra also had a late night. In her case the initial cause was her sister who came to ask a question.

'What do you look for in a man? What will it take for you to fall in love?'

'What brought on that question?'

'I just wondered. Since it is impossible to measure love, how do you know that you are in love.'

'Are you trying to determine if you are in love with Sir Marcus?'

'Sir Marcus? No, of course not. He is wonderful to talk to, but falling in love with him? I am sorry, Alexandra, but whatever gave you such a ridiculous idea?'

'You and he seemed to take great pleasure in each other's conversation and company.'

'Oh. That. It is simply that, for a man, he is reasonably intelligent.' Daphne shrugged off the suggestion.

'Reasonably intelligent?'

'Well... he is not my equal, but he is quite bright.'

'I suppose from you that is high praise indeed.'

'It certainly is. But you did not answer my question. What will it take for you to fall in love?'

Alexandra was thoughtful for a minute, as she tried to put her feelings into words. 'I suppose I want a man who accepts me as I am. A man, who is not intimidated by my rank, but also does not expect me to become a good little wife. You know, the kind that most men seem to want, obedient to their every whim and without an opinion of her own.'

'Are you not a little harsh?'

'Perhaps. But think of Mr Clifford. What kind of a wife do you think he wants?'

'One who is obedient to his every whim and has no opinions of her own.' Daphne sighed. 'I must admit, I only ever really thought about it in the abstract, but that man has made it personal for me. I really do not wish to marry.'

'Do you not want children? Most women do.'

'I like puppies and kittens, but babies... no thank you. You know, when you have to go away, I visit the tenants on your behalf. Every time one of the women has a baby, they all expect me to want to hold them, but I can never get out of the house fast enough. What about you, Alex? Do you want children? I mean children for the sake of having children, not because you need an heir.'

Alexandra smiled softly. 'Yes, I do want children, and no, not because I need an heir.'

Daphne hugged her sister. 'Well, I hope you find the right kind of man to give you those children, as well as the respect and acceptance which you need.'

~~H~~

After Daphne said good night, Alexandra lay awake for a long time.

She acknowledged to herself that she was in love with Marcus. While she thought that he had become attached to her sister, and the feeling seemed mutual, Alexandra was determined not to interfere.

But now that she knew that Daphne had no interest in the gentleman, it left the field open for herself.

Had not Aunt Beatrice said that friendship was the best basis for a marriage? She was now determined to see if friendship could be turned to love.

Perhaps the love she felt for Marcus would be enough for both of them, she thought for a moment. The next moment she chided herself. That was not a good premise for a marriage. She was not some desperate female who needed a husband on those conditions.

Alexandra wanted an equal. Not necessarily in the eyes of society, but an equal in character and in love.

She thought about how Marcus always treated her with simple respect. He did not fawn or flatter, and he did not try to appear superior to herself. He was a good conversationalist, who listened to her opinions, and when he disagreed with them, he was prepared to discuss their differences.

She had once seen him when he was out riding. His horse had spooked, nearly throwing him. Instead of disciplining the horse, as many would have done, he had gently soothed it.

The housemaids all reported how polite and considerate he was, and once Alexandra accidentally overheard them comment on his physical appearance in quite inappropriate, but most flattering, terms.

Thinking about it, in the privacy of her chambers, Alexandra was prepared to agree with them, even compliment them on their excellent taste.

No, she would not settle for second best. But if she could change their friendship to love, she would have the man, who she thought would be her ideal partner.

She gave a soft chuckle. Her family names were most appropriate, and she would live up to them.

The hunt was on.

~~H~~

18 *Confrontation*

After yet another failed attempt to engage the gentleman in a conversation, which touched upon subjects which were more personal, Alexandra was ready to scream in frustration and confusion.

He side-stepped, avoided, prevaricated or was perhaps genuinely obtuse.

What was she doing wrong? Or was she doing everything right, and Marcus simply was not interested? Damn propriety, which insisted that it was wrong to speak openly about one's feelings. Or at least it was improper for women to do so.

If she spoke, would being too forward chase Marcus away?

If she did not speak, would she ever discover how he felt about her?

Her education had focused on running the estate and the Earldom. She thought that while she had perhaps not mastered every aspect of her duties, she was confident that on the whole she was doing a good job.

And yet, when it came to personal matters, she was fumbling around in the dark. All the confidence she had when dealing with business matters, escaped her when it came to matters of the heart.

What was the right thing to do? Should she speak or be silent? Alexandra was at the point where she wanted to throw things and beat her head against a brick wall.

~~H~~

It had started so well. Arriving at the stables to go for her morning ride, she had encountered Sir Marcus saddling his own horse. Seizing the opportunity, she had invited him to join her on the ride.

'Sir Marcus, tell me about your family. Do you have any siblings?'

'I have but one much older sister. My parents were greatly relieved by my arrival since our estate is entailed to the male line.'

'Was your sister greatly disappointed to learn that she could not inherit?'

'Thankfully, not at all. She told me that even from a very young age, all she ever wanted was a husband and a houseful of children.'

'In that case, your sister is the exact opposite of mine. I suspect that the main reason she has no interest in marriage is, that she does not like children.'

Without considering the implications, Marcus asked, 'what about you, Lady Alexandra, do you like children?'

'I do indeed. While I may be in an unusual position due to my circumstances, I do still have many of the same interests as the majority of my sex.'

Realising that he was straying into dangerous territory, Marcus changed direction and teased, 'I must compliment you; you are exceedingly proficient in hiding your love of lace and fripperies.'

'You have my father to thank for this. He abhorred over-ornamentation, and even though my mother's taste was more elaborate, she acquiesced to his preferences. In many ways I believe they were quite mismatched, but my mother accepted my father's eccentricities, and they appeared to be happy.'

Marcus used this comment to relate anecdotes about the eccentricities of several acquaintances, and for the rest of their ride, avoided awkward subjects.

~~H~~

That outing set the tone for all their other encounters.

Alexandra often invited Marcus to join her for walks. Whenever possible she invited him to sit next to her at meals. She engaged him in conversation whenever the opportunity arose. All to no avail.

Admittedly, Alexandra was treading a fine line. She was trying to engage the gentleman as much as possible, but without making it seem as if she was hunting him.

When they had gone for walks, he had politely offered his arm, which she had been happy to accept. They spoke about many things.

Alexandra was pleased to discover that their tastes were very similar in many respects. They had the same core values. She was able to discuss the issues she had with some of the men, who were uncomfortable in having to deal with a woman in her position.

Sir Marcus had been open-minded, easy to talk to and sympathetic. But he had never taken any of the opportunities to direct the conversation to the subject she most cared about.

Marcus always emphasised his delight in their friendship.

Alexandra was ready to strangle him.

~~H~~

After yet another frustrating day, Lady Alexandra retired for the evening and changed out of her formal attire into a comfortable dress she used for lounging in her rooms.

She was curled up on a sofa in her sitting room with a book to try and forget about her irritation with Marcus, when she heard a commotion in the corridor before someone was hammering on her door.

When she pulled the door open, she saw the maid Jenny with her hand raised to knock again. Her other arm was being grasped by none other than Lord Bassington.

Jenny looked somewhat dishevelled and one of her sleeves was torn.

'What is the meaning of this?' demanded Alexandra, although the tableau in front of her was rather obvious.

'Nothing to concern yourself over, Lady Alexandra,' replied Lord Bassington. 'I was just reprimanding your maid for sloppy and unsatisfactory service.'

Jenny gave him a disgusted look, before turning to her Mistress. 'Lady Alex, the unsatisfactory service His Lordship is complaining about, is my refusal to warm his bed.'

'I gather you were rather persistent about it?' Alexandra asked the... young man.

'So what. That is part of her job. But would you believe she had the temerity to kick me in the shins,' complained Bassington.

'Well done, Jenny. Please send two footmen to me,' requested Lady Alex of the maid, who wrenched her arm from her accuser's grip and stormed off.

'Well done? How can you condone such behaviour from your staff? To attack a guest in your house,' exclaimed the outraged Lord.

'I do not condone attacks in my house,' explained Lady Alex.

'Good. I expect you to fire the little wildcat.' Lord Bassington looked satisfied. Since the little wretch would not do his bidding, he wanted to be revenged for her slight towards him.

'You misunderstand, Bassington. I do not condone guests, who are enjoying my hospitality, to repay me by attacking my staff whilst under my roof.' Lady Alex, glad to have a legitimate target on whom to vent her frustration, gave him a look that should have turned him into an icicle.

Before Bassington had a chance to protest, Lady Alex saw two of her largest footmen arrive. 'Perkins, Smith, please take Lord Bassington to his room and ensure that the servant's door is locked. His Lordship will remain in his room for the rest of the night and leave at first light.... Oh, and ensure that no female staff enter his quarters.'

Bassington looked at her in horror. 'You would evict me for expecting my rights from a servant?'

'You have no rights to help yourself to my servants. I employ the maids as maids, not as whores to entertain my guests.' Alexandra was furious with the man. He had seemed charming and good company. Now he was showing his true colours. While she had considered him as a potential suitor, she would never tie herself to a man who would treat anyone in this way.

Hearing that kind of language from the lady shocked Bassington to sobriety. During his visit he had seen a charming and witty young lady, whom he thought to charm into marriage, in the expectation that she would give him access to her wealth. Now he saw the strong Master of the Estate and realised that even if he had succeeded in wooing her, he would never have been in charge.

To a man who liked to have his own way, that would have been unbearable. He was only grateful that no one had witnessed his humiliation.

He had obviously done his dash, therefore there was only one thing to do to salvage some shred of reputation. Bow out gracefully. 'My apologies, My Lady. Your standards are very different from the ones I am used to. I will not trouble you with my presence again. Thank you for your hospitality. Goodbye, Countess.'

'Goodbye, Lord Bassington.'

Perkins and Smith, who had been waiting behind the gentleman gave each other satisfied looks. Their respect for Lady Alex had always been high, but now it climbed even further. She not only protected her staff but was prepared to face down the entitled son of a Duke.

Perkins, the more volatile of the two, almost hoped that the gentleman would try to give them some trouble. He would enjoy teaching him the error of his attitude. Since Lord Bassington went with them quietly, Perkins assumed that his lordship was a bully, who would only ever pick on somebody smaller and weaker.

No matter, by morning he would be gone.

~~H~~

Unbeknownst to the participants in this drama there was another witness after all.

Sir Marcus had been relaxing in his room thinking about his hostess.

This visit was both bliss and torture. He enjoyed the opportunity to spend so much time in Alexandra's company. The walks with her holding his arm. The conversations about anything and nothing in particular. The way she smiled at him. He felt privileged that she considered him her friend. He treasured every moment.

At the same time, it was also torture since he could never have her. It was out of the question. She needed to marry someone of her own station, not some minor Baron. Albeit a wealthy Baron, although most people were not aware of that fact, but still only a Baron.

He understood that this house-party was designed to help her choose a husband. He could not fault the selection of the young men who had been invited. According to their pedigree, any of the others would make a suitable consort for the Countess.

At the moment he was simply grateful that the lady had wanted the company of her friend.

He had taken off his coat and shoes and was lounging by the window when he heard a commotion in the hallway.

When he exited his room to investigate, he was just in time to see Bassington limp around the far corner of the hall. Being ever curious, Marcus followed Bassington to the family wing, where he heard frantic pounding. He was just in time to see Bassington grab hold of an obviously unwilling maid.

He was about to make his presence known when the door to the Master's suite opened and Lady Alexandra took charge of the situation.

Sir Marcus was impressed yet again by the polite but firm way in which the lady dealt with the incident. She was not cowed by Bassington's bluster. While most men would have been horrified to see a woman act in such a forceful manner, Marcus was delighted.

How he longed to have her by his side.

But he could never be more than just her friend. He could not aspire to her station and her wealth. Society would not allow her to connect herself with someone of his rank.

If she did, there would be malicious gossip about their relationship. While he did not care a pin about what people said about himself, the thought of this wonderful lady being maligned was intolerable to him.

He returned to his room feeling as conflicted as ever since discovering her identity.

~~H~~

At breakfast, the next morning the other guests noticed the absence of Lord Bassington. When Lady Cordelia commented on the missing gentleman, Lady Alex explained casually, 'apparently, Lord Bassington received a message last night that forced him to return home post haste.'

Sir Marcus, who had just taken a sip of his coffee, almost choked on his drink. But his coughing at least covered his laughter which tried to escape him. *The clever minx*, he thought, *she is telling the complete truth and nobody except I and the footmen know that she was the one to deliver the message.*

He glanced across the room where he had noticed Perkins earlier. The man swiftly turned and busied himself with the items on the sideboard, but not before Marcus spied a slight smirk on his face.

~~H~~

19 Courtship?

Lady Alex was at her wits' end. She could not make any headway with Sir Marcus.

Eventually she remembered her father's advice. If you have a problem which you cannot solve, ask for help. The obvious person to help was Aunt Beatrice.

The same evening, after their guest had retired, she went to see Lady Beatrice. 'Aunt, I need your help,' she said reluctantly.

'I was wondering when you would come to me.'

'You knew I needed help? Am I so very obvious?'

'Not at all, but I know you better than our guests. You are interested in Sir Marcus, are you not?'

'Yes, I am, but I cannot establish if he feels anything for me other than friendship.'

'I suppose that you would like me to find out how he feels.'

'Yes, Aunt. I would be most grateful if you could.'

'What if he only does feel friendship towards you?'

Alexandra sighed. 'In that case I will have to reconsider my future. I do not wish a marriage of unequal affection.'

'Perhaps if he knew how you feel...'

'No, Aunt. Please do not tell him that I am pining for him. I could not bear the embarrassment. I also do not wish for him to offer for me out of some feeling of obligation. I refuse to settle for second best.'

'That is a very fine line you want me to tread.' The lady hugged her niece. 'I will do my best.'

Alexandra gave her a tremulous smile. 'Thank you.'

~~H~~

A few days later, Lady Beatrice had a chance for an accidental seeming private conversation with Sir Marcus.

They chatted pleasantly, until Lady Beatrice enquired, 'I have noticed that you are spending much time with my niece. I hope you will not take it amiss if I ask your intentions.'

'I find Lady Daphne to be a fascinating conversationalist. She has a unique view on many subjects.'

'That was not the niece I was concerned about.'

'Lady Beatrice, please rest assured that I would never do anything to harm Lady Alexandra.'

'Sir Marcus, I know that you are intelligent enough to know that this house-party was intended to give all of you young people a chance to get to know each other, to see if you might be compatible with an eye towards marriage.'

Marcus could not suppress a small smirk as he replied, 'please forgive me if I say that, considering the composition of the guest list, it does not take exceptional intelligence to discern the intent of this visit. I am grateful to have been included, as it has been a privilege to become better acquainted with both your nieces. I must say that I am very grateful to have gained your niece's friendship.'

'Friendship you say?'

'Indeed, Lady Beatrice. I greatly admire Lady Alexandra and am proud that she considers me her friend.'

Something in the way that Sir Marcus expressed himself did not ring quite true to Lady Beatrice. But no matter how much she prodded and prompted, Sir Marcus was adamant in his admiration and friendship which he felt for Alexandra.

Eventually, the lady conceded defeat. As much as it hurt her on her niece's behalf, it seemed that Alexandra was correct in her evaluation of the gentleman's feelings.

She hoped that it would not take her niece too long to get over the disappointment of her hopes.

~~H~~

Sir Marcus was about to excuse himself, when their conversation was interrupted by the entrance of the butler, carrying a salver.

'Pardon me for interrupting, but an express has just arrived for Sir Marcus.'

Lady Beatrice waved at the gentleman. 'Go ahead, read your letter. It must be urgent.' As she stood, to give him privacy, she noticed the black edge on the envelope.

Marcus too, had noticed the black edge, giving some warning of the content. He broke the seal and quickly scanned the message. He stood for a long moment; his face contorted in pain.

When he looked up, he noticed Lady Beatrice watching him with concern and sympathy. 'I am sorry, Lady Beatrice, but I must leave. My sister…' he trailed off, waving the missive.

'You have my sympathy, Sir Marcus. Of course, you must go to your family. I will make your apologies to everyone.' She turned to the butler, who had waited discreetly in the expectation of just this order. 'Have Sir Marcus' luggage packed and his carriage readied.'

Once the butler had gone, she asked, 'might I enquire…'

Marcus sighed. 'She died delivering her ninth child, a daughter, apparently.' He shook himself out of his reverie. 'My Lady, I thank you for your exquisite hospitality. I hope to see you again under better circumstances.'

'Safe travels, Sir Marcus. I too hope that we shall meet again when circumstances permit. Know that you are always welcome in our homes.'

Sir Marcus bowed to the lady, and with a final farewell left the room to ready himself for the journey, while Lady Beatrice made Sir Marcus' apologies to all their guests, but without going into details.

~~H~~

Earlier in the day, Lady Alexandra had been informed that Tom Bourke, one of her tenant farmers had had an accident.

She immediately sent for the doctor and set out to assess the situation for herself. When she arrived with Larkin, who usually accompanied her, she discovered that Mr Bourke had been replacing some shingles on the barn roof, when he had slipped and fallen. In the process he had broken his leg.

She sent Larkin back to the house to fetch one of the men to help out while the farmer was unable to work.

The doctor arrived at the same time as Larkin returned with the news that Mrs Martin would send the requested assistance, as well as a maid to help care for the farmer.

After the briefest of greetings, the doctor examined Tom Bourke. 'It is just as you said, Mr Bourke, the leg is broken. But you are lucky, it is a clean break.' He looked around and ordered, 'Larkin, you are just the man I want. Hold onto Bourke while I set the bone.' More politely he requested, 'My Lady, if you could take Mrs Bourke outside…'

Mrs Bourke, a woman in her late twenties, was kneeling beside her husband, holding his hand while quietly weeping. Alexandra coaxed her to stand and accompany her out of the cottage. On the way, Alexandra noted that the woman was heavy with child.

'What's going to become of us,' the woman whispered, as Alexandra encouraged her to sit on a bench beside the porch. 'Tom won't be able to work, and I can't do much right now.' She placed a protective hand on her abdomen, her tears flowing freely now. 'And the doctor. We had saved up a bit for the babe, but without the doctor, Tom's leg won't be fixed.'

'Mrs Bourke, do not worry. I have sent for someone to do your husband's work while his leg heals, and Mrs Martin is sending a maid to give you a hand with the house and him.'

'But we cannot pay for them,' exclaimed Mrs Bourke, her eyes opened wide in panic.

'You do not have to. Mr Brown, my steward, told me that your husband is a hard worker, exactly the kind of tenant we like to have. I want to be sure that he has a chance to heal properly, so that he can continue to work once he is fully recovered.'

That information brought a teary smile to the woman's face. 'My Lady, I don't rightly know how to thank you. I was so worried, not just about Tom, I must admit, but about myself and the babe. I'd heard that when tenants can't work, they usually get turned out. And Tom and I only got married less than a year ago when we moved here.'

'Well, worry no more. Doctor Carstairs is a good doctor, and I am certain that your husband will be fine. In the meantime, just take care of yourself and the babe.' Alexandra smiled and patted the woman's hand. Spotting some towelling, she fetched it and handed it to Mrs Bourke to dry her face.

They looked up as the doctor and Larkin came looking for them. 'Mrs Bourke, I have set your husband's leg and splinted it. He needs to stay off it for several weeks. I will bring some crutches when I check on him in a couple of days. But as long as he is careful and does as he is told, he should be back on his feet in no time.'

'Thank you, doctor.' Mrs Bourke stood. 'Please forgive me, but I must see to Tom.' She dipped an awkward curtsy and rushed into the house.

Alexandra rose to her feet as well. 'Is he going to be well?'

'I never lie to my patients... or their families,' the doctor smiled. 'As I said, it was a clean break which was relatively simple to set. Although it was helpful to have Larkin to assist. But I must be going, I have another patient to see.'

~~H~~

On the way back, Alexandra considered what she had witnessed. The way Mrs Bourke worried about her husband and her child, made her think that the couple had married for love.

This thought inevitably made her think of Marcus. Since she had been called to the Bourke farm, she had not seen him today. She also had not seen her aunt, making her wonder if Aunt Beatrice had had a chance to speak to the gentleman.

She suddenly felt exasperated. She was tired of wondering and she was tired of not having answers. Alexandra determined to find out the truth as soon as she returned.

Since Lady Beatrice was not in the drawing room, Alexandra went to look for her in the Mistress' suite. This too she found empty.

Exasperated, she stormed into the Master's suite and with Sally's help she had a quick bath to rid herself of the smell of horse. As soon as she was properly dressed, she stalked to the guest wing, to the door of Sir Marcus' room.

She wanted answers and she wanted them now.

Alexandra did not even get a chance to knock on the door, since it was wide open, and several maids were busy cleaning the room and putting covers on the furniture, as they always did when a room was to remain unoccupied for any length of time.

It appeared that Sir Marcus had left the building.

~~H~~

It took Alexandra a further ten minutes to track down Lady Beatrice, who informed her and Daphne of Sir Marcus' departure and the reason for his hurry.

Alexandra, distracted from her own concerns, commented, 'Sir Marcus was very fond of his sister. It must have been a great shock to him.' She shook her head. 'The poor lady. To have safely delivered eight children…'

As Alexandra trailed off, Daphne interjected, 'You have just given me yet another reason why I have no intention of marrying. I do not like children in the first place but risking my life to bring another squalling brat into the world, is an excellent reason to remain celibate.'

'Daphne, have you no compassion?'

'I do. I feel dreadful for Sir Marcus' poor sister. But I cannot help but think that perhaps eight children would have been enough.'

'I believe that she wanted a daughter since all the other children were boys.'

Daphne sighed. 'I just hope that nobody will make the girl feel like she killed her mother. That should not be a burden any child should have to carry.'

'Did anyone ever make you feel guilty about the fact that your birth prevented mother from having more children?' Lady Beatrice asked, concerned about the distraught expression on Daphne's face.

Daphne nodded, and whispered, 'Grandmother Hunt.'

Lady Beatrice hugged Daphne. 'I know I should not speak ill of the dead, but my mother had some exceedingly silly ideas. She did not think that women had the ability to be anything but wives and mothers. She considered it her duty to produce an heir and a spare. When I was born, she could never reconcile herself to the idea that I was a girl, and that she would be unable to have any more children. Fortunately, neither of your parents suffered from that affliction. They loved you and did not care if you were male or female.'

'You understand.'

'Yes, I do. I would also like you to consider, if you had a younger brother, do you think he could do as well as Alexandra as Master of Herne? He might have grown up as a wastrel like many of the other so called noble sons.'

Daphne managed a weak grin. 'I suppose I did the Earldom a favour.'

~~H~~

Now that Sir Marcus was gone, Alexandra noticed that she had a shadow.

Mr Andrew Reddington's father owned a small estate in Kent, which his oldest brother was to inherit. Having to earn a living, he was studying law in London.

Alexandra had met him at several balls and dinners, and had found him pleasant, if insipid, company. He had been invited as a potential match for one of the other ladies, but he seemed to be fixated on his hostess.

As soon as Sir Marcus had absented himself, Mr Reddington saw his opportunity to woo the elusive Countess.

Even though he preferred town hours, he rose early enough to accompany Lady Alexandra on her morning rides. He was amazed when he discovered that the lady was taking the ride not only for the pleasure of the outing, but also to check on her tenants.

At mealtimes, he took the seat formerly occupied by Sir Marcus, and entertained the lady with what he considered to be amusing anecdotes about some of the cases with which he had dealt.

Mr Reddington seemed impervious to Alexandra's attempts to change the subject to less disparaging topics.

It seemed that wherever Alexandra was, Mr Reddington was not far away.

The day before the scheduled end of the house-party, Mr Reddington took the opportunity of the morning ride to address a subject dear to his heart.

Unlike many solicitors, he came to the point immediately and did not waste unnecessary words. 'My Lady, I believe that my attentions have been too marked for you not to realise my devotion to you. I think you the most beautiful and accomplished lady of my acquaintance, and I would be honoured if you would allow me to officially court you.'

'Mr Reddington, while I am flattered that you think so highly of me, I do not believe that we would suit.'

'My dear lady, having had training both in estate management and in law, I believe that I would make you a most supportive husband. With me by your side, you would not need to trouble yourself with such mundane tasks as are required to properly manage an estate. You would be able to devote yourself to such tasks as are the preferred purview of ladies.'

'And what are those tasks that you believe to be suitable to the feminine temperament?'

'Why, embroidery and perhaps painting screens, when you are not busy managing the house and nurturing your children. And as for outings, you could confine yourself to pleasure rides on a gentle mare with a proper side-saddle.'

'As I said, Mr Reddington, I do not believe that we would suit, since I enjoy managing *my* estate and I despise embroidery and painting. As for riding, a prefer Pegasus, who can outrun any other horse we have so far encountered.'

'But surely, you would not expect your husband to be subordinate to you?'

'Not at all, Mr Reddington. I expect my husband to be my partner; each of us taking care of our own responsibilities.'

'But that goes against the natural order of creation. You cannot expect a man to accept such a situation.'

'That is why, Mr Reddington, I said that we did not suit.'

~~H~~

Eventually, the time for the visit came to an end, a situation for which Alexandra was exceedingly grateful.

It looked like the house-party had been a partial success, since three couples were now courting.

Lady Theresa was being officially courted by Lord Paul Sanderson. The gentleman was quite tall and powerfully built; he was a gentle giant, who gave an impression of great strength and calmness. He had taken one look at the shy young lady, and all his protective instincts had come to the fore. Lady Theresa in return, had immediately responded to the security he offered. Her parents, seeing their daughter comfortable in the gentleman's presence, were delighted with the potential match.

Mrs Mornington's nieces also had potential suitors, which pleased both her and Lady Beatrice.

Regrettably, the gentlemen for whom Lady Beatrice had the greatest hopes to partner her niece, all had to leave for one reason or another. She was starting to get worried that her niece might have to settle for a marriage of convenience.

~~H~~

20 Winter of discontent

Alexandra was grateful for the peace which reigned in Herne Hyde once again now that the guests had gone.

Lady Beatrice was busy catching up on correspondence which she had neglected during the visit.

Daphne and Amelia were once again to be found in their laboratory, or in the house perusing the latest scientific papers which had recently been delivered.

Alexandra threw herself into her own work. The harvest was just starting and keeping her busy.

She also made a point of visiting all her tenants, to ensure that all was well with them. She perhaps spent more time at the Bourke farm than the others. Mr Bourke was doing well, although he fretted at being confined to his bed. The only thing which made him obey the doctor's orders was the threat that he would be crippled for life if he re-damaged the leg.

Once he was allowed out of bed, he was busy building a crib and other small items for the baby.

The first day he was standing on his own feet without the aid of crutches coincided with the birth of his son. Mr and Mrs Bourke requested permission from the Countess to name the boy Alexander.

Lady Alexandra was touched by the request and readily agreed.

~~H~~

The weeks slipped past, and the harvest was finished. Unlike for many other estates, it had been a good harvest, even if not the best. It was good enough that no one beholden to Alexandra would go hungry over the winter.

Despite this, Alexandra was restless. She wanted to speak with Marcus but had to respect his mourning period for his sister. By the time it was acceptable for him to have visitors, winter had set in with a vengeance, making travel difficult.

Correspondence between them was not an option. Apart from the fact that it would have been completely improper, what Alexandra wanted to discuss could only be done in person.

She had no option but to wait for the next season to travel to London, and hope that Marcus too would decide to visit town.

Needing to keep busy over Christmas, Alexandra devoted herself to the paperwork associated with the estate. She also found time for reading and practice sessions with Mr Martin.

When the weather permitted, she went for rides on Pegasus; on days of bad weather, they exercised in the indoor arena.

Slowly but surely the new year arrived.

~~H~~

Sir Marcus had just completed the finishing touches on his latest project. He was closing up the barn which he had converted for his experiments, when he noticed a storm blowing in from the southeast.

He had returned to Vintington Vale after his sister's funeral, grateful for the three-month mourning period, which allowed him to come to terms with his loss. Marcus had been using this time to focus on his experiments with steam.

He hurried back to the house, entering through the backdoor, when he heard a familiar voice in the foyer, asking, 'is Sir Marcus at home?'

He called out, 'I certainly am, Robert,' and made his way to greet his friend.

'My apologies for barging in unannounced, Marcus. I was on my way to Bristol, but that storm which is following me looks like it is in a hurry to get there before I can. I was hoping to impose on you to put me up until it blows over.'

Marcus was pleased to have his friend's company and instructed his housekeeper to ready a room for Lord Robert Flinter.

While the room was being prepared, Marcus invited Robert into the library for some mulled wine to take off the chill.

As they entered, Robert commented, 'I must be more chilled than I thought, because this room feels like it is baking.'

'You are chilled, but not as much as you might think. This happens to be one of the warmest rooms in the house.'

'Are you not afraid that with that many open fires, you will not set those books alight?'

'Which open fires?' Marcus grinned and waved an arm, indicating that not a single fire was in sight.

Robert looked around. 'I cannot see a pot-belly stove either.'

Marcus led his friend to a tiled structure, with a seat attached, near his desk. 'If you want to get warm, that is the best place.'

Robert gingerly touched the tiles, and after a moment pressed both hands against them. 'Ahh. That is more like it. Hot enough to do some good, but cool enough that you can touch it, unlike a metal stove. What is it?'

'It is called a cocklestove. A small fire inside heats the bricks. With this stove you do not have ashes, smoke, or cold drafts from the chimney in the room. I have started to convert the whole house to this kind of heating.'

'Is there one in my room?' Robert asked hopefully.

'There is, but the fire is only just being lit. If we had known you were coming, it could have been lit earlier and come up to temperature.'

'Damn. I suppose I just have to thaw out here.'

'This might help.' Marcus handed a cup of steaming mulled wine, which one of the servants had just brought, to Robert, who took it and sat down on the bench around the stove.

'Ahh. That is just what I needed,' he sighed after the first sip.

'So, why are you off to Bristol at this time of year?' Marcus asked, taking a chair opposite Robert, and putting his feet up onto the bench to warm them.

'Sorry, I am not at liberty to say. I should not even have mentioned my destination. I suppose my brain was frozen with the cold.'

'If you cannot talk about your travels, tell me about your family. How is Alistair?'

Glad to be able to change the subject, Robert happily related the latest attempt at compromise which his twin had escaped.

~~H~~

Once the housekeeper announced that Lord Robert's bath was ready, the men separated to get warmed and cleaned up, before meeting again in the library before dinner.

Since it was just the two of them, Robert was agreeable to dine there, rather than the dining room, which had not been heated. Over dinner, Marcus explained, 'it seems ridiculous to me to heat the whole house just for myself. When I am inside, I spend most of my time in the library or in bed. It seems such a waste to heat the other rooms when I never use them.'

'You are turning into quite the hermit. But I noticed that you are still tinkering with ways to improve this big pile.'

Encouraged by his friend, Marcus explained the work which had kept him busy in recent times.

The food, while simple, was plentiful, as well as hot and tasty. Since the weather was cold, they continued drinking the mulled wine. By the time they finished eating, they both had imbibed a significant amount of alcohol and were feeling quite relaxed.

They moved to the comfortable chairs by the cocklestove, propping their feet up on the bench.

The friends chatted pleasantly until Robert asked, 'how was your summer? I hear that you spent some weeks at Herne Hyde.'

'It was a pleasant visit. I especially enjoyed meeting Lady Daphne. She has an exceptional mind.'

'So Lady Alex tells me. But she sounds too highbrow for my liking. I find the sister much easier to talk to.' Robert was watching his friend without being obvious about it. Seeing a pained expression cross Marcus' countenance, he provoked his friend. 'I hope I get a chance to call on her, next time I am in London.'

The response was unexpected. 'When will you marry her?'

'Marry Alex? Are you out of your mind? Why would I want to marry her?'

'Because she is in love with you.'

'Alex in love with me? Now I know that you are out of your mind.' Robert laughed uproariously but stopped suddenly as he started to have hiccups.

When he recovered, he explained, 'Alex is a wonderful girl, but she is much too abrasive for me. I like my girls to be softer, less driven. Oh, I admit I like her spunk, but marrying her? I would be safer with a hedgehog.'

'How dare you insult Alexandra.' Marcus surged out of his chair unsteadily and waved his fists. 'I will teach you not to speak about her in such an ungentlemanly manner.'

'You would fight me for the lady's honour?' Robert chuckled.

'I will not let you insult her. Now get up.'

'If you insist.' Robert carefully put his cup on the table, barely missing the edge, and suddenly launched himself at Marcus, throwing him off-balance.

Since both men had indulged heavily in the mulled wine, neither was steady on his feet, and they crashed to the floor, where they grappled with each other, rolling about. Marcus was ineffectually trying to hit Robert, who happened to be on top, when his friend started to laugh again.

'You are in love with her!' exclaimed Robert, catching Marcus' fist, admittedly by accident. 'That is why you cannot bear to hear a word against her.' He pushed himself off Marcus and plopped onto the floor next to his prostrate host.

'What I feel is irrelevant,' huffed Marcus, as he, in turn, tried to sit up.

'It is very relevant. Why do you not tell her?'

Marcus looked sheepish. 'She is a Countess, and I am just a lowly Baron.'

'You poor sap. Do you really think she cares about rank?'

'Perhaps not, but society does care. And while I may only be a Baron, I do have some pride. I will not be labelled a fortune hunter.'

'So, to salve your pride, you prefer to be miserable for the rest of your life.'

'But she deserves so much more than I can offer.'

'Marcus, has it ever occurred to you that Alex does not need more rank or wealth. She has rank and wealth in abundance, and with those she has independence. The independence to marry as she pleases.'

Robert waited for his friend to reply but noticed that Marcus was not yet convinced. He added with a smirk, 'the only things she does not have are intangibles… such as love. Would you deny her that?'

This comment startled Marcus. 'I had never considered things from that perspective,' he admitted at last. 'I need to think about this… when I am not foxed.'

~~H~~

A few days later, the weather cleared sufficiently for Robert Flinter to continue his journey.

Marcus was grateful that Robert had enough sensibility to avoid the subject of Lady Alexandra for the rest of his stay.

Once he did not have to worry about entertaining his friend, Marcus did sit down to consider Robert's ideas.

He still thought that the lady was out of his league, and he had nothing to offer her. While it was true that he had nothing in a material sense to offer, he could offer his love and respect.

Marcus had claimed that he was afraid of being perceived as a fortune hunter, but that was not quite true. It was only the smallest part of the whole picture. Most everyone who knew him, was aware that financially he was extremely comfortable. Some of those inventions which he had tinkered with for years, turned out to be very commercially successful.

Even his knighthood was earned before he inherited the barony. Which was why he preferred to be known as Sir Marcus, rather than Lord Scott, Baron of Vintington.

No, the truth of the matter was that he was afraid that Alexandra would reject his suit, and in the process, he might also lose her friendship.

But what of the lady?

Could she have feelings for him? He remembered every instance during the summer when he was in her company. Her face always lit up when they met.

He had been telling himself that it was simply that she enjoyed his company as a friend. But could it be more?

Marcus considered that in their society it was not acceptable for women to make the first move. They were expected to wait for a man to make his preference known.

Alexandra had mentioned that due to her unusual position in society, she had to be extra careful about her actions, and how they might be perceived. She did not wish to alienate herself from her peers.

Could she be waiting for him to declare himself?

There was only one way to find out.

~~H~~

21 Reciprocity

1806

Lady Alexandra was frustrated yet again, or perhaps still. Her interactions with Sir Marcus had been confusing. He had usually been reserved, acting with all due propriety and as a platonic friend. But sometimes she thought that she detected a spark of something else.

Eventually, just when she had decided to speak to him candidly, he had received an urgent message Inducing him to rush to his brother-in-law's estate without even saying goodbye to her. Since then, due to the dictates of propriety, she was not able to correspond with the gentleman, she had to wait until she saw him again.

When her aunt suggested a brief visit to Town, Alexandra was in favour of the distraction, especially as she hoped that the gentleman would also attend the season.

Within days of her arrival in London, Lady Sefton paid her a visit and insisted that she simply had to come to Almack's for their next ball.

~~H~~

Since Alexandra did not have a polite reason to refuse the invitation, she decided on a small subterfuge.

She arrived at Almack's in company of her aunt, having an ankle bandaged and using a walking stick.

'My dear Lady Sefton, I could not miss this ball to which you have so kindly invited me, although I am afraid that I will be unable to dance.'

'My dear Lady Herne, I do hope you were not injured rescuing another small boy from a large folly.'

Alexandra laughed at the reminder. 'Not at all. It was merely a careless move on the stairs. I will be perfectly recovered in a few days... as long as I do not engage in any strenuous activity.'

Alexandra spent a few hours chatting with the other guests. Her supposed injury allowed her to avoid the more persistent gentlemen. Every time one became too assiduous in his attentions, she introduced him to another young lady.

She became quite popular with her supposed rivals, with perhaps the exception of Miss Simpson, who cooed insincerely, 'it is such a shame that you cannot participate in the dancing tonight, Lady Alexandra. I do hope that you will not be incapacitated too long. It would be such a shame if you missed your chance to catch a husband for yet another season.'

'Do not trouble yourself on my behalf, Miss Simpson. Unlike most ladies, I have no need to catch a husband.'

'But do you not wish to be well settled and Mistress of your own home?'

'Since I am already the Mistress of my own home, as well as the Master of my estates, I believe that I am quite well settled,' Alexandra smiled innocently at the obnoxious young woman.

Her friend, who was better informed than Miss Simpson, urgently whispered into her friend's ear, 'Lady Alexandra is the Countess of Herne in her own right. She has more status and wealth than you could ever aspire to.'

Alexandra was blessed with exceptionally acute hearing, and caught the gist of the whisper, but gave no indication of having heard the advice, instead she pretended to be interested in watching the dancers.

Meanwhile, Miss Simpson coloured an interesting shade of red, although it was uncertain whether it was due to embarrassment or jealousy. At last, she managed to grate out, 'I congratulate you on your good fortune, Lady Alexandra.'

'Thank you, Miss Simpson. I must confess I find it an exceedingly pleasant circumstance that I can attend a ball purely for the pleasure of the company in general, without any other concern.'

'You are fortunate indeed.' Miss Simpson managed a tight smile at the reminder that she was desperately trying to catch a husband, who could provide her with the kind of lifestyle to which she would like to become accustomed. Such as Lady Alexandra already enjoyed.

~~H~~

Alexandra was in the ladies' retiring room to adjust the bandage which was starting to come loose. Since she did not wish to be observed in her activity, she had chosen a spot behind a screen in the furthest corner of the room.

She was bent down, adjusting the wrapping, when she heard two ladies enter. She was about to sit up and make her presence known when she heard them mention Lord Denmere. Something in the tone of voice induced her to keep quiet.

She was glad that she did, as Miss Simpson thanked her friend for providing the sleeping draught which she planned to use to incapacitate Lord Alistair, the Marquess of Denmere, and getting him into her bed. Since Alistair had a reputation for being honourable, Miss Simpson was looking forward to being the next Duchess of Denton.

Alexandra kept as quiet as she possibly could, until the two women left.

Soon after, she joined her aunt. 'I need to find out where Lord Denmere is to be tomorrow, and get an invitation to the same event,' she told Lady Beatrice quietly. Seeing the quizzical look, she added, 'I will explain later.'

By noon the following day, Lady Beatrice had not only been informed of the threat to their friend, but she had also arranged for an invitation to Lord Sulwood's dinner party that night.

~~H~~

Alexandra was chatting with her friend, Lady Cordelia, at Lord Sulwood's house.

'You were lucky not to be in our area the other week. We had the worst snowstorm in years,' Lady Cordelia told Alexandra. 'We were quite snowed in for several days.'

'How terrible. I hope no one was caught out in the storm.'

'No, we were all quite safe. Although I heard that Sir Marcus had an unexpected visitor who sheltered for the duration of the storm.'

'How is Sir Marcus? Is he still mourning his sister?'

'I believe he is quite recovered. He indicated that he was considering coming to Town. Although it could be several weeks before he arrives. He needs to oversee some repairs.'

Lady Cordelia watched Alexandra light up when she imparted that news. She wondered what it would take for these two to work out that they were perfect for each other.

~~H~~

When Alistair arrived, she rushed up to him and gushed, 'Lord Denmere, how lovely to see you again. I have not seen you in much too long. So many things have happened. You simply must call on us so that we can have a nice long chat.'

Alistair was happy to see his old friend again, but there was something in her manner that gave him pause. She was not normally this effusive.

'It would be my greatest pleasure to call on you at any time, my Lady,' he replied in the same vein. Then he asked in an undertone, 'What is wrong?'

'I will tell you all tomorrow. In the meantime, be careful of Miss Simpson,' Alexandra replied in the same way while he bowed over her hand. 'In that case, you simply must come to tea tomorrow afternoon. My aunt will be thrilled to see you again. She was saying just yesterday that it was such a shame we have not seen you lately.' She babbled on, again at full volume.

After a little more meaningless chatter, Alistair turned to Lady Sulwood, who had been delayed by Miss Simpson.

'Ah, there you are Lord Denmere. I am thrilled that you accepted my husband's invitation,' gushed Lady Sulwood. 'Have you met all our other guests? No? Let me introduce you. We should have a charming evening. We have such diverse guests.' Their hostess proceeded to suit her actions to her words.

When everyone went in to dinner, Alexandra was pleased to note that Alistair was seated opposite her. She was less pleased that Miss Simpson had been placed next to him. At least Alexandra could keep an eye on the pair.

During dinner, Alexandra had an interesting discussion about the current political situation. Mr Courtenay was pleased to inform her about the Ministry of Talent which had been instituted by Lord Grenville.

At the end of dinner, when the ladies rose to retire to the drawing room, Alexandra's route took her past Alistair and Miss Simpson, who was having trouble with her reticule. The port had been poured by the time she untangled it from the lace of her gown. She appeared to become so flustered that she dropped the reticule as she rose to leave.

Alistair, ever the gentleman, bent to pick it up for her.

Since Miss Simpson's hand had come too close to Alistair's port, Alexandra pretended to stumble as she walked past him, just as he was trying to hand the object to its owner. Her seemingly reflexive grasp to catch herself from falling, jostled his arm, which in turn sent the reticule on a collision course with his glass of port.

Alexandra appeared mortified. 'Lord Denmere, Lord Sulwood, I must apologise for my clumsiness. Maybe the wine was a little strong for me. I am not normally so unsteady.'

'No harm done, my Lady. There is nothing broken, and there is plenty more port.' Lord Sulwood assured her.

'You are too kind, my Lord.' She raised a hand to her forehead. 'I believe a cup of coffee with the ladies will set me right. Miss Simpson, shall we join the ladies?' She politely asked the other lady, who had again taken possession of her reticule. She then took Miss Simpson's arm and led the lady out of the dining room.

After that excitement, the evening seemed interminable. Alexandra was grateful that Alistair was ready to leave at a reasonable hour.

~~H~~

At two o'clock the following afternoon, Alistair presented himself at Hunt House. He was shown into the family parlour, where he was greeted by Lady Beatrice and Lady Alexandra.

Both appeared anxious to see him. 'I hope nothing untoward has befallen you since last night?' asked Lady Beatrice.

'I am perfectly well. What is this all about? Why are you so anxious?' Alistair was puzzled.

Both ladies smiled in relief. Lady Beatrice explained. 'Alexandra overheard a conversation to the effect that Miss Simpson is trying to compromise you. We had heard that she was to be at the dinner last night. Alexandra managed to get herself invited to give you warning.'

'But I could not go into detail while there was a chance we might be overheard.'

'Can you give me the details now? Miss Simpson seemed quite harmless when I met her last night. She is not a lady I could ever be interested in, but she did not seem desperate enough to force a compromise.'

'The day before yesterday I was at Almack's. While I was in the lady's retiring room, I was sitting down and fixing one of my shoe roses, when two ladies came into the room.' Alexandra told him mendaciously since she was not going to explain the pretended injured ankle. 'Since it was not obvious that I was present, they discussed a plan of putting a sleeping draught into your port and then placing you into bed with Miss Simpson. Unfortunately, I do not know where or when.' Lady Alexandra explained.

'I was rather concerned that when we were getting up to move to the drawing-room. Her hand was very close to your glass.'

'Was that why you jostled my elbow and made me spill it?' Alistair asked concerned. 'I know that you are not usually so clumsy or prone to fainting.'

'I am more prone to feinting of a different kind.' Alexandra grinned. 'Although I am not certain that it was necessary under the circumstances, I did not wish to take a chance. She may try elsewhere.'

'I would assume it would be at a private function.' Alistair mused. 'Otherwise, they will not have access to a bedroom. Do you know where she is staying? She mentioned last night that she was only visiting London.'

'I heard her mention a Cousin George, but I do not have a surname,' Alexandra replied.

'Maybe for the foreseeable future, I should not accept invitations by anybody named George until we find out where she is staying. But why did you not simply send a note?'

'As you well know, Ladies are not supposed to correspond with men to whom they are not betrothed. It was also somewhat nebulous, and I truly did not wish to put that sort of information into a letter.'

She now grinned, 'although I was quite prepared to make a scene if you did not leave on your own feet last night.'

'I appreciate your concern, but I would not want to place you in an untenable position. And although I like you well enough, I do not wish to marry you.'

'Ever the charming gentleman,' Lady Beatrice teased.

'You know perfectly well that I think of you as two of my best friends. I simply have no wish to marry a friend, who is only a friend. And you never know, one of these days Alexandra might meet someone she wishes to marry. It would be a shame if she were shackled in a marriage already.'

'Aunt, you know well enough that the feeling is mutual as far as Alistair is concerned. I have someone else in mind.'

'You do? Who is the lucky man and when should I congratulate you?' Alister asked with a relieved grin.

'His name is irrelevant since he does not yet know. He is proving rather myopic.' Lady Alexandra shrugged. 'But there is no hurry for me. You, on the other hand, need to ensure that you are on your guard. It is a pity that Robert is away again. He makes such a wonderful decoy.'

Lady Beatrice chimed in, 'ladies are rarely interested in younger sons. Especially when they appear not to have a title or fortune.'

'Robert is very happy that the family decided on keeping his prospects very quiet. I only wish I had had the same opportunity,' sighed Alistair.

'It must be terrible to be so very desirable,' teased Lady Beatrice. 'Console yourself, it's a Duke's life, but someone has to do it.'

~~H~~

22 Advice

It had been a month since the dinner at Lord Sulwood's house and Alexandra had still not heard anything from Sir Marcus. She wondered how extensive the needed repairs were, or whether he had changed his mind about coming to Town.

She was still debating what to do when she received an unexpected visitor.

'Your Grace, it is an unforeseen pleasure to see you again,' Alexandra greeted the Dowager Duchess of Denton.

'I wanted to thank you for the assistance you provided to my grandson. It was exceedingly well done.'

'There is no need to thank me. Your grandsons and I have a pact to save each other from the pitfalls of society. I just hope that Miss Simpson decides to refrain from her attempts in future.'

Alexandra arranged for tea to be served and the ladies settled for a chat.

The Duchess was pleased to inform Alexandra about new developments. 'It appears that when Miss Simpson became tired of waiting for a chance at Alistair, she chose another quarry. The gentleman in question did not even need much persuasion to sample her charms.' The Duchess related the tale with a certain relish. 'Unfortunately for her, when she cried compromise, he laughed at her. She is only lucky that he has no interest in spreading the story beyond his own circle.'

The Dowager Duchess paused for effect. 'It seems she thought that if she could not be Alistair's wife, she would be his mother.'

'Miss Simpson tried to compromise the Duke of Denton?' Alexandra exclaimed with a laugh.

'Indeed, she did. I suspect she now regrets that action. He has never considered marriage after his wife died.'

They continued to converse pleasantly for a few minutes, until the Dowager Duchess suddenly asked, 'how do you feel about Sir Marcus?'

Alexandra was caught off-guard by the blunt question. 'I... ah... find him excellent company,' she managed to prevaricate.

'That is not what I asked. Do you love him?'

'What business is it of yours to ask such a question?' Alexandra responded with some asperity.

'My dear girl. I am an old woman. I do not care to beat about the bush. I need to know if you love Sir Marcus.'

'Why do you need to know?'

'I will answer your question if you answer mine... honestly.' The Dowager fixed Alexandra with a gimlet stare.

Alexandra looked the Duchess in the eye as she considered her answer until she declared firmly, 'yes, I do.'

'Good. That solves one problem.' The impish smile which the Duchess sported, would have been more suitable for a street urchin.

'I have answered your question. Will you now answer mine?' Now it was Alexandra's turn to be adamant.

'I have it on very good authority that Sir Marcus is hopelessly in love with you. But that silly boy suffers from nobility. He believes you are too far above him, and is determined to suffer in silence, so that you can marry someone of your own station. Like my grandson Robert.'

'Robert?' Alexandra laughed. 'As you know, he is more like a brother to me.'

'I know. I also know that Robert feels the same way about you. Therefore, he wants you to be happy.'

'I appreciate Robert's sentiments. But why are you telling me this?'

'Because Robert asked me to speak to you. According to him, Marcus will never offer for you due to his misplaced humility. He suggests that if you love Marcus, you will have to speak to him. He also advises the use of a mace, or at least a large stick, to beat some sense into Marcus' thick head. Subtlety will not work.' The Duchess grinned as she passed on the advice.

'I had considered this option, but was afraid that if I spoke openly, it would chase him away, and I would lose all chance at a future with him.'

Alexandra sighed. 'There is also such a thing as propriety. All my life I have been taught that men get to make those kinds of choices and react badly when a woman usurps what they consider to be their rights. Even the daughters of Dukes do not propose to men.'

'That is generally true. But you are in an unusual position. The daughter of a Duke may have a courtesy rank equal to a Marquess, but she has no power. You have the rank, the title, and the power. Use it.'

Alexandra grinned. 'Does anyone ever win an argument against you?'

'Not if they know what is good for them,' the Duchess answered in the same tone of voice. 'I am gratified that we understand each other.'

Both ladies shared a quiet laugh.

~~H~~

Marcus was chafing at the need to oversee the repairs to his estate. The storm which had brought Robert to his door, had also caused significant damage to several tenant houses and barns, as well as a bridge.

It had taken weeks to effect all the necessary repairs, and while his steward would have been able to supervise, Marcus felt it was his duty to take care of his tenants personally.

Of course, he was not procrastinating, he told himself. It was simply that his tenants had priority over his personal preferences.

But eventually, everything was put to rights. He made a final inspection before returning to his manor, looking forward to a long hot bath and a meal. Afterwards he would relax for the rest of the day and tomorrow he would head for London.

He was uncertain whether the imminent interview made him feel elated or filled him with dread.

~~H~~

Alexandra exited her carriage and walked up to the door, which had opened, and declared to the footman, 'I am the Countess of Herne, and

I need to speak to Sir Marcus.'

The footman was too startled by the imperious demand, that he stepped aside and wordlessly led her to the library. As he opened the door, he found his voice. 'The Countess of Herne is here to see you.'

Marcus rose from his chair by the window at the announcement. Before he could say anything, Alexandra pushed past the footman and closed the door in his face.

Taking her courage into both hands, she marched towards Marcus, stopping barely an arm's length from him.

Using the proverbial stick, and without preamble she declared, 'I love you and I want to marry you.'

Marcus was dumbfounded. 'You what? What did you say?' he stammered.

'I love you and I want to marry you.' Alexandra repeated carefully.

'Are you serious?'

'I have never been more serious in all my life,' Alexandra grated through clenched teeth, holding onto her temper and her tears of frustration as well as embarrassment, by the slightest of margins.

The reality of the situation was starting to sink in as Marcus stared at the determined face of the lady he loved. Lost for words, he responded by taking a step forward and pulling Alexandra into his arms.

His kiss, which he intended to keep to a gentle brush of his lips against hers, inflamed his senses, and within moments, all the pent-up passion he had felt for Alexandra broke through his barriers.

Giving himself up to the sensation, he had only enough awareness to note that not only did he not receive a slap, but Alexandra was responding in kind.

When they broke from their kiss and caught their breaths, Alexandra asked with shining eyes, 'I gather the answer is yes?'

'I should not, but yes, if you truly want me... I would be proud to accept your hand in marriage.'

'After a kiss like that, you do not really have a choice but to accept the rest of me as well.'

'But you do know that it is a bad idea, do you not? Society expects you to marry someone of similar rank.'

'Society can go hang. But speaking of rank... You do know the law regarding titles...'

'You mean that when we are introduced it will be as the Countess of Herne and the Baron of Vintington.'

'Does that bother you?'

'Should you not have asked this question before you bludgeoned me into accepting your proposal?'

'Was that the reason you did not propose to me?'

'No. I just thought you deserved someone better than me.'

'Better than you?'

'You know, like Robert Flinter, or even his brother.'

'I love Robert... like a brother. The idea of marrying him, feels simply wrong.'

'So, you did think about marrying Lord Robert Flinter?'

'Naturally. I considered every single man of the nobility and the gentry, who is of an appropriate age. Some of them I like well enough... as friends, but not as a husband. Lord Robert and his brother fall into that group. But none of them are you.'

'But I cannot understand what you see in me,' Marcus still protested.

Alexandra smiled mischievously. 'I will be happy to explain to you in detail... when we have a spare year or two.'

Marcus shook his head trying to understand, saying, 'but...' only to be stopped by another kiss.

When they eventually stopped kissing in favour of breathing, he conceded, 'I believe that you suffer from insanity, but since I love you too, I am prepared to enjoy the consequences.'

Alexandra drew herself up to her full height. 'I do not suffer from insanity,' she protested in mock indignation, before breaking into a grin. 'I thoroughly enjoy it.'

Since he could not refute her logic, Marcus settled for another kiss.

~~H~~

A loud grumble interrupted them.

As they broke apart, Alexandra explained with a chagrined smile. 'I was too nervous to eat on the journey.'

Marcus laughed. 'I am relieved to hear that I am not the only one who dreaded proposing.'

'You were planning to propose? To whom?'

'To you, My Lady. As soon as I arrived in London.'

'And when, if ever, did you plan to go to London?'

'Would you believe tomorrow?'

'Truly?' When Marcus nodded, Alexandra huffed. 'Does that mean I wasted this journey?'

'Not at all. I am most grateful that you took the burden of the proposal off my shoulders.' He smirked. 'And I shall always treasure the look of determination you wore. Apart from that, I shall have a story to tell our children and grandchildren, of how the love of my life, against all the dictates of society, proposed to me.'

Before Alexandra could reply, her stomach protested its emptiness again. 'I think I had better call for some food, otherwise I will not have the opportunity to tell the story if you die of hunger.'

Marcus rang the bell to ask for some food to be brought.

The butler entered only moments later and with a rigorously suppressed smile informed his master, 'the countess' companion has suggested that the countess would be hungry. Dinner will be served momentarily in the dining room. I have also taken the liberty to prepare the blue suite in the guest wing. The lady will join you in a moment.'

At the mention of her companion, Alexandra exclaimed, 'oh,' and reflexively clapped a hand over her lips.

Marcus turned to Alexandra with a quizzical expression. 'I forgot all about her,' she exclaimed blushing furiously.

'I thought you might, which is why I took the liberty of making arrangements for dinner and our stay. I hope that you are not offended, Sir Marcus.' The lady appeared behind the butler.

'Lady Amelia, I am so very sorry...'

Marcus turned towards the newest intruder. No, not intruder, distinguished guest, he corrected himself as he recognised the lady. 'Your Grace, welcome to my home. I am honoured by your visit.' Marcus was proud of his quick recovery.

'I could not let my young friend travel without a proper chaperone. Apart from that, I needed to make certain that you children did not make a complete... bungle of this.'

Alexandra regained her composure and smiled as she declared, 'I think we managed to handle the situation rather well, Lady Amelia. Sir Marcus and I are engaged to be married.'

'Congratulations. It is about time.' The Dowager Duchess of Denton smiled with real warmth at the news.

A footman arrived to inform the party that a meal was ready to be served. As soon as he had delivered the message, he hurried below stairs to bear the glad tidings, although some less generous souls might have called it gossip.

~~H~~

23 *Acceptance*

Over dinner, the Duchess explained her presence, allowing Alexandra to make up for the meals she had been unable to eat on the way, due to the anxiety she had felt.

'Since I bludgeoned Alexandra into proposing, I thought it prudent to come along, to ensure that propriety was observed. I did not want the old biddies to have a chance to question the nature of your attachment.'

'I doubt that anyone in society would have the temerity to question anything which you sanctioned, Your Grace,' Marcus responded with a smile. He was still rather bemused that not only did Alexandra love him, but one of the leading doyens of society had actively promoted the match.

The Duchess chuckled. 'Not if they know what is good for them. I know where too many bodies are buried.'

'I certainly cannot argue with that sentiment,' Marcus admitted with a grin. He had met the formidable lady only twice before and had found her to be rather intimidating. According to Robert, he was not alone in feeling this way.

Now that the Duchess was on his side and being helpful, she portrayed a very different character. He would almost call it mischievous.

Perhaps the lady could help with a problem which had concerned him. 'I must confess that I have been worried about how society will react if Lady Alexandra were to marry someone outside her social circle.'

'There will be weeping, wailing, and gnashing of teeth,' the Duchess said with relish. 'It is not because you are unworthy, but because the others were found wanting.'

Alexandra, who had assuaged the worst of her hunger, took the time to interject, 'most of the men I have met over the last three years wanted to marry me for my title and my wealth. They thought that since I was young and female, that I was also uneducated and gullible.'

The Duchess murmured sotto voce, 'you mean stupid and malleable.'

Alexandra ignored the comment and added gleefully. 'They were shocked when they found out I was quite aware that many of the normal rules for marriage do not apply to me.'

While she took another bite of her dinner, Marcus asked, 'you mean like the fact that you maintain your title and control of your estates?'

'That and the small issue that my husband does not even have automatic access to the income from the estates. They thought that they could charm or bully me into handing over control to them.'

Marcus gave a soft chuckle. 'I am glad that I have known you long enough to be aware that you do not suffer fools. I suspect that if you had shown even part of the fire I can see, most of those suitors would have run for the hills.'

'You mean that by being polite I extended my suffering?' Alexandra asked in mock horror, raising the back of her hand to her forehead dramatically.

The Duchess shook her head in amusement. 'Your aunt is a wonderful lady, but I could have better taught you how to use the power you have.'

'I am most grateful that you did not, Your Grace. I might have been too terrified of your protégé,' Marcus quipped.

'Are you terrified?' Alexandra was astonished.

Marcus shrugged. 'Robert called you abrasive and implied that you were intimidating. But I cannot see that in you. I always thought of you as sweet and gentle.'

'You thought of me as sweet and gentle after you watched me break Frederick's wrist?' Alexandra exclaimed in disbelief.

'Frederick?' questioned the Duchess.

'The late unlamented Earl of Marven.'

The Duchess laughed. 'That is a story which I must hear.'

Marcus was happy to oblige the lady, while Alexandra finished her dinner.

'While that was not the kind of power I was talking about, I am glad to hear that you can look after yourself. With that attitude you two should not have any problems.' She stifled a yawn.

'I am afraid that being bounced around in a carriage for a day has exhausted me. I suggest that tomorrow we discuss how to introduce your forthcoming marriage to society. It will also allow me to rest for a day before being subjected to another carriage ride.'

On her way out of the room she had a final comment. 'Keep the door open.'

~~H~~

Alexandra and Marcus exchanged a startled glance before giving way to relieved and slightly hysterical laughter.

'The Duchess is a force of nature,' declared Marcus with a shake of his head.

'Indeed, she is,' responded Alexandra with a fond smile.

'But she has reminded me of my duty as a host. You too have spent the day travelling...'

'Yes, I have, but while I am tired, at present I could not sleep.'

'In that case, shall we return to the library? It is more comfortable.'

Since Alexandra was agreeable to the suggestion, he offered her his arm to escort her back to the library, where she requested coffee as she looked around.

'This room is just as I imagined it from your description.'

Once the coffee had been served, Marcus poured a small measure of brandy, which he offered to Alexandra. 'This might help settle your nerves to help you sleep later.'

When she gratefully accepted the drink, he poured himself a slightly larger one and sat in a chair near his lady. It was a heady thought... his lady.

'May I ask you a question?' he asked.

'You just did,' Alexandra teased as she took a small sip of the excellent brandy.

Marcus pretended a fierce scowl at her facetious remark. 'Very well. I shall ask another one. Please do not misunderstand, I am thrilled that you asked me to marry you, but I do not understand... why me?'

'Because I love you.'

'But you have everything. You are intelligent, beautiful in every way, you are a great conversationalist and wonderful company. You are accomplished in many areas. You have all that, not to mention wealth and a title in your own right. You could have any man you wanted and yet you chose me.' Marcus looked as confused as he felt.

Alexandra was perplexed. 'I confess that I cannot understand the contradiction in your character. You always struck me as being confident in who you are. Why would you think yourself unworthy of me?'

'Did you not listen to all the things I just listed?'

'You do not give yourself enough credit. You are intelligent, well read and good company.' She let her eyes roam over him from head to foot with a teasing smile. 'You are also easy on the eyes and an excellent dancer. The fact that you resisted asking me to marry you tells me that you are not interested in me for my position or wealth.'

She smiled and grasped his hand, giving it a little squeeze to emphasise her point. 'But most of all, you accept me as I am. You seem to like me as a person and are not trying to change me.'

Alexandra sighed. 'Do you know how rare it is for a man not to be intimidated by me. Or worse, there are those who are offended by my audacity to have a mind of my own. And even worse still for them, I do not need them, and I do not kowtow to their perceived superiority.'

'Robert accepts and respects you,' offered Marcus.

'Yes, and I love him for it... like a brother.' She smiled and shrugged her shoulders. 'I know that on paper, he would be perfect for me, but I cannot think of him as a husband.'

'I am greatly relieved. I would hate to be compared to my friend at inopportune times.'

'You will just have to ensure to capture my full attention.' She smiled at Marcus and finished the last of her coffee and brandy. Before she could say anything else, she yawned. 'I believe the brandy has done its job,' she declared ruefully.

'In that case, I shall not keep you from your well-deserved slumber.' He rose and offered his arm again. 'If you will allow, I shall conduct you to your chambers.'

Alexandra gratefully accepted his arm. The eventful day was catching up with her at last. It felt good to be escorted by Marcus.

When they reached the door, he leaned towards her for a brief brush of his lips against hers. 'Sweet dreams, my love.'

His prediction came true. Alexandra did have the most wonderful dreams of their future together.

~~H~~

Two weeks later, the Duchess' plan came to fruition. She hosted the engagement ball for Alexandra and Marcus. Her reasoning was that she had the larger house, which could accommodate the mere two hundred of their closest friends with greater ease. She did not say that few people would dare to decline an invitation from her.

The time had been hectic. As soon as they returned to London, the Duchess met with Alexandra and Lady Beatrice to discuss the guest list and issue invitations.

Marcus attended this meeting and was amused as well as awed by the discussion. He now understood Robert's irreverent nickname for the Duchess... General of Denton or GoD for short.

'We want all the most influential people who have no axe to grind about this marriage. If you have the support of half the Dukes and Earls in the kingdom, the rest will fall into line.'

The Duchess turned to Marcus. 'I suppose it would not hurt to invite the Prince, since he is the reason for your knighthood.' She smiled impishly at his stunned expression.

'How do you know...'

'What can I say, people like to tell me things.'

'Lady Amelia, while I agree with most of your choices, there are a few people I would like to invite. They may not be powerful, but they are my friends,' Alexandra declared, politely but firmly. 'And I believe that Marcus would like to invite his friends as well.'

The Duchess was taken aback by that statement but recovered quickly. 'Please forgive me, my dear, for getting carried away with my scheming. Of course, you must invite your friends. May I suggest that you and Sir Marcus discuss your personal guest list, while your aunt and I will take care of the official one.'

'You mean the officious one,' muttered Marcus.

The Duchess grinned. 'Touché.'

~~H~~

Alexandra and Marcus moved to the other end of the room to compile their list of guests.

Before they started, Alexandra asked, 'you never did tell me about your knighthood. How did that come about?'

Marcus looked embarrassed as he realised that he would have no option but to confess. 'About six years ago, I had been to a dinner with friends and decided to walk home. I saw a man, who seemed to be under the weather, being attacked by what I thought to be footpads and went to his assistance. There was something of a scuffle and most of them ran away. I found out later that the man was a member of the royal family.'

'Something of a scuffle and only most of them ran away?' Alexandra asked suspiciously.

'Well, I was armed and one or two were incapable of running,' Marcus admitted uncomfortably.

Alexandra squeezed his hand as she chuckled. 'No wonder you were not bothered by what I did to Frederick. But who was the man?'

'I promised not to say. My knighthood is simply for *Services to the crown*.'

'I see. Very well, I shall not press you. Now shall we start? I need to arrange for Daphne and Amelia to come to Town. And I would like to invite the Cartwrights. They are lovely people.'

The spent the rest of the afternoon telling each other about their friends and writing invitations.

~~H~~

The day of the ball arrived and everyone who could attend had accepted the invitation. The day before, the official announcement had been published in the papers.

The Dowager Duchess of Denton and the Countess of Marven, Lady Amelia and Lady Beatrice to their friends, were part of the receiving line with Alexandra and Marcus to greet their guests. It turned out that very few introductions were necessary.

Once most of the guests had arrived, they moved to the ballroom where Alexandra and Marcus led the first dance.

While another couple took their turn, Alexandra asked, 'it is quite official now. I hope you have no regrets?'

'The only regret I have is not asking you a year ago.'

'You do realise there is a severe punishment for procrastination.'

'There is?'

'We could have been married for a year already...'

Marcus groaned. 'That is indeed the worst punishment imaginable. I am only grateful that you did not insist on a long engagement.'

'I saw no reason why I should be punished for your mistake,' she teased. 'I waited long enough.'

'I just wish it was already next month.'

~~H~~

Halfway through the evening there was a stir at the door, as a late arrival made his entrance. Having been forewarned of this occurrence, the Duchess as well as Alexandra and Marcus had stationed themselves near the entrance to the ballroom.

When the Prince was announced, a hush fell over the room as everyone bowed or curtsied. The Duchess greeted their august visitor but before she could go further, the Prince turned to Marcus. 'It is good to see you again under such happy circumstances.'

'Your Royal Highness, you honour us with your presence.'

'Think nothing of it. If it were not for you, I would not be here and since I was curious to meet this unusual Countess whom you plan to marry, I thought I would briefly stop by.'

Marcus performed the introductions.

'I must congratulate both of you to have chosen so well,' the Prince announced graciously with a smile. 'I hope that you will have a long and happy life together.'

The couple thanked him and after a few more words, the Prince took his leave.

As soon as he had gone, conversations erupted around the room. 'The Prince approves...' 'How did Sir Marcus meet the Prince?' 'I did not realise that he was so well connected...'

The Duchess covered her glee with a pleasant mask, as she quietly said to the couple, 'I told you so.'

Alexandra and Marcus looked at each other and simultaneously rolled their eyes and grinned.

~~H~~

24 Conclusion

During the four weeks leading up to their wedding, Alexandra and Marcus dealt with various legal and personal issues.

To ensure her sister's security, Alexandra transferred the title of Dianadale to Daphne. When she informed her sister of the gift, Daphne asked cheekily, 'are you trying to get rid of me so that you and Marcus can have some privacy after you marry?'

'Not at all, and you know it. I simply want to make certain that you will always have a home of your own, where you can do as you please. You and Amelia might become two eccentric old ladies together after all, conducting research into whatever takes your fancy.'

'It might be an idea to set up our laboratory there, so that when you have a brood of children, Amelia and I can escape.' Daphne hugged Alexandra. 'You truly are the best sister that I could wish for.'

The other issue to solve as living arrangements.

Marcus, ever practical brought up the topic one evening when he was having dinner at Hunt House. 'You do know that if you were a conventional wife, I would expect you to come live with me in my home.'

Alexandra who had not even considered leaving Herne Hyde, looked stricken. Before she could formulate a reason for remaining at her home, Marcus reassured her. 'You are fortunate that I have considered this situation, and even more lucky that I have no great attachment to Vintington Vale, since it used to be my uncle's home. While I have improved it, to me it is simply a house.'

The sheer relief which washed over Alexandra's features made him chuckle.

'But what about your estate?' she asked.

'My steward is excellent and has taught me about estate management since I never expected to need the knowledge until I inherited the title unexpectedly. Occasional visits will be all that is required, and your estate is not so far that I cannot visit whenever I am needed.'

'You have considered everything,' Alexandra congratulated him. But a moment later she looked at Marcus in consternation before switching her gaze to Lady Beatrice.

Her aunt laughed. 'I wondered when it would occur to you that you are currently occupying the Master's suite while I am enjoying the luxuries of the Mistress' suite.' Lady Beatrice looked at Daphne, who nodded vigorously.

'Daphne suggested that on consideration she would like to live at Dianadale and would like to have my company. We will be close enough to visit regularly.'

'And I can set up a new laboratory where Amelia and I can work. Which would leave our current facilities available to Marcus.' She grinned at him. 'Call it our wedding present to you.'

Marcus, who had not thought of that aspect of relocating to Herne Hyde, appreciated his almost sister's gesture.

When the couple had a moment alone after dinner, Alexandra suggested, 'I hope you will not mind sharing my rooms until yours are redecorated to your taste. And we can call all the combined chambers the Master suite and be done with it.'

'I would much prefer to share your chambers even after the redecoration,' Marcus commented suggestively.

Alexandra blushed but fervently agreed.

~~H~~

The wedding was almost anticlimactic. It was a small affair and only family and their closest friends were invited.

By chance, or possibly due to some arm twisting by a certain Dowager Duchess, Robert Flinter was on a short leave in London, to stand up with Marcus on that special day. He had arrived the day before and gone to visit his friend.

'I am glad to see that Alexandra managed to beat some sense into you,' he teased after their greeting, sporting a huge grin and clapping Marcus on the shoulder.

'No beating was required, but I understand that I have you to thank for spurring Alexandra to propose.'

'I simply suggested that my grandmother should have a word with the lady and explain your predicament... congenital stupidity and excessive humility. It just so happens that most people find grandmother irresistible.'

'I suspect that Alexandra will develop that same quality,' mused Marcus.

'I am certain of it. Which is why I am glad that she had her cap set on you and you are the one to marry her. She would be forever ordering me about.'

'I have not noticed any tendency of her trying to give me orders.'

'Naturally not. You are much more sensible than I am.'

Marcus laughed. 'You are quite correct. And to prove it, I will ask you to leave immediately... after dinner. I have a big day tomorrow and I need to be rested.'

Robert gracefully bowed to the request, although not without suggestive comments about why Marcus would need his energy.

~~H~~

The wedding was held at St George's and even though the official wedding party was small, the church was nearly full of onlookers.

Most of the onlookers, and even a few of the invited guests were shocked when Alexandra walked into the church and up the isle unaccompanied by anyone. Daphne, her bridesmaid, was already waiting at the altar.

She could have been accompanied by a regiment of dragoons or a troupe of jugglers, and Marcus would not have noticed. He had eyes only for his bride, who looked radiant and proud as she walked up to him, looking for all the world as if she were claiming her prize.

Archbishop Langton, who had offered to perform the ceremony, had agreed to forego the question about who would give Alexandra away, as well as leaving out the word obey from their vows.

Marcus, although aware of the plan, could not help but murmur with a smile, 'independent to the end?' as Alexandra gave him her hand.

The Archbishop gave Marcus a withering look as he started the ceremony. 'Dearly beloved...'

Neither Alexandra nor Marcus paid much attention to the ceremony, although they managed to respond appropriately when required.

It seemed to be but the blink of an eye when they signed the register, and the Archbishop announced, 'I am pleased to introduce to you Lady Alexandra Hunt-Scott, the Countess of Herne and Lord Sir Marcus Hunt-Scott, Baron of Vintington.'

Amidst the cheers of the audience, the newly married couple claimed each other with a kiss which although brief and chaste, was full of a promise of passion.

~~H~~

The wedding breakfast had been held at Hunt House

The food, the wine and the company were excellent. Robert's speech was memorable because despite its brevity it was full of impudent advice and innuendo, and put both the bride and groom to the blush.

Their guests were understanding and considerate, making their farewells before the couple became too impatient.

Even Lady Beatrice, as well as Daphne and Amelia said their goodbyes. The Dowager Duchess had invited the ladies to stay with her for a week, giving Alexandra and Marcus privacy at Hunt House.

Once the guests had gone, Marcus took his wife into his arms and teased, 'what shall we do now? I suppose we could go for a walk, or perhaps you would like to read a book?'

'None of those things. There is something in my rooms which I would like to show you,' Alexandra suggested with a blush.

When they entered her, no... their, rooms, Alexandra firmly shut the door behind them and turned to Marcus, who asked, 'what did you want to show me?'

'This,' she murmured, as she snuggled into his arms and kissed him.

The passion which they had suppressed for the last six weeks was at last allowed free rein. It was already the early hours of the next morning by the time they fell into an exhausted sleep.

Shortly after dawn, Alexandra roused briefly. Seeing the relaxed face of her new husband, she smiled contentedly as she snuggled up to him. Just before she drifted back to sleep, she murmured happily, 'mine.'

~~H~~ ~~H~~ ~~H~~

Epilogue

Like most couples, fortunate enough to marry for true love, Alexandra's and Marcus' lives were mostly happy.

They did not always agree, but they managed to work out their differences.

Against the Hunt family tradition, they had two sons as well as two daughters.

They petitioned the crown to allow Marcus' title to go to their second son. A petition which was gladly granted by the Prince Regent.

~~H~~

Daphne and Amelia also got their wish. They enjoyed a long and happy life conducting research, unencumbered by such tedious things as husbands and children.

Lady Beatrice shared their house and ensured that Daphne and Amelia remembered to eat.

The only unexpected aspect of their life was the cat which adopted them.

~~H~~

Books by Sydney Salier

The Denton Connection

Don't flatter yourself – A P&P Variation

Mrs Bennet's Surprising Connections – Prequel to 'Don't flatter yourself'

It's a Duke's Life – Sequel to 'Don't flatter yourself'. A P&P spin-off

Unconventional

An Unconventional Education (Book 1) – A P&P Reimagining

Unconventional Ladies (Book 2) – A Regency novel inspired by P&P

P&P Variations

Don't flatter yourself – Revisited – The alternate version of this P&P Variation

Consequence & Consequences – or Ooops – A Regency Romance inspired by P&P

Mr Bennet leaves his study – A Regency Romance based on P&P

No, Mr Darcy – A Regency Romance inspired by P&P

Remember – you wanted this – A collection of P&P variations

Surprise & Serendipity – A P&P Variation

You asked for it – A P&P Variation with a twist

www.ingramcontent.com/pod-product-compliance
Ingram Content Group UK Ltd.
Pitfield, Milton Keynes, MK11 3LW, UK
UKHW041638190726
13854UKWH00006B/2564

9 798464 829237